The

Saint in the Cellar

Laura Vosika & Chris R. Powell

Gabriel's Horn Publishing

Cover Design: Laura Vosika

Contact editors@gabrielshornpress.com

Published in the United States by Gabriel's Horn Press

First printing: 2022 Printed in the United States.
For sales, please visit www.gabrielshornpress.com

ISBN: 978-1-938990-77-9

Other Books by Laura & Chris

The Blue Bells Chronicles: a tale of time travel
- *Blue Bells of Scotland*
- *The Minstrel Boy*
- *The Water is Wide*
- *Westering Home*
- *The Battle is O'er*

Food and Feast in the World of the Blue Bells Chronicles: a gastronomic historic poetic musical romp in thyme

Tales of Things Beyond Our World: stories of the supernatural

The Path that Shines: a story of life, love, and loss

The Four Spheres: habits for a better life

Glenmirril Garden: original music in the style of Celtic jigs and reels (with Judd Knauss)

Go Home and Practice: a record book for music students and musicians for better progress

On Wings of Light and Love: poetry and essays on love

Gabriel's Horn Poetry Anthologies, collator/editor
- *Startled by JOY: 2019*
- *Startled by NATURE: 2020*
- *Startled by LOVE: 2021*

The

Saint

in the

Cellar

Laura Vosika
& Chris R. Powell

I have begun to tell of things that I could not bring to any end even if I had a thousand tongues of steel and talked until they were all worn out.

– Sawles Warde

PROLOGUE

The wilderness is the solitary life of the anchorite's dwelling, for just as in the wilderness there are all the wild beasts, and they will not endure men coming near but flee when they hear them, so should anchorites, above all others, be wild in this way...

– Ancrene Wisse

Anthony knelt in his cell before the Crucifix, contemplating the words of the *Ancrene Wisse* and his purpose in this wilderness—to hold himself away from the world as a wild beast held itself beyond the danger of humans and other predators. There was no danger from a world one avoided—even fled from.

Of course, he had not fled. He had come here at the request of James and Helen Long. They had been gone for decades and their grandchildren no longer wanted such a big, old house. But he must still be needed here, or God would have called him home. He had not.

So Anthony waited and prayed, *God's Will Be Done*, as realtors came through the house. He knelt in prayer in his cell as the voices of potential buyers spoke in the Garden Room outside his walls.

He smiled to himself as he thought of that beautiful room, visible through the bars when he opened his window. How often had Mr. or Mrs. Long sat there, conversing with him, among the green plants Helen had so lovingly tended. Anthony smiled at the irony! Most would not consider a mansion on Summit Hill to be a wilderness. For him, it was.

"The house was built in 1889 for James and Helen Long. He was a railroad baron who moved to St. Paul in 1871."

Faith listened with half an ear to the history of the 7,500 square foot mansion, its fourteen rooms and mahogany, oak, and maple woodwork; to the history of the family who had lived here. The incredible entry hall—which was really a room unto itself—had already sold her, with its massive, ornate fireplace.

She glanced into the Garden Room. It had a white stone floor and windows set in the top third of the walls that spilled light into the basement. Plants thrived on tables set around the walls. "Who takes care of these?" she asked.

"I think the grandson of the Longs comes over regularly. This was originally where the laundresses worked—but you can see it makes a wonderful greenhouse. And you can go from here straight out to the back garden." The realtor indicated a door that opened to steps leading up to the yard. "The yard is perfect for hosting soirees. There's a fountain and a view to die for at night of the bridge and the city."

"Mm." Faith left the room and moved down a hall with exquisite mahogany panels to the big room at the end. It could be a bedroom, a workroom, almost anything. It didn't matter.

"There are some really wonderful people living on Summit Avenue," the realtor said, as Faith looked around the room. It had plants, windows set high, a bed, a shelf with books on it. "There's a state supreme court judge within a few houses of here, and one of the CEOs of Gander Mountain and the author of the *Dragon of Dinis Powys* books."

"M.M. Love?" Richard asked.

"Yes, him."

"Those are the books Jacob's friend likes so much," said Richard.

"Aren't they being made into movies right now?" Faith asked.

The realtor nodded eagerly. "You'd have some really neat people for neighbors. Great people."

"What do you think, Faith?" Richard walked the length of the big room. "With the cold winters here, this would be a great place for Jacob to ride his bike."

"Mm." She wished she'd had such a place as a child. "Can you imagine the parties we can host here? That entry—the front room? That huge fireplace!" She smiled. "We'll have to get to know our neighbors and host them!"

Anthony looked up from his prayers. The woman's voice came through the walls. It would be strange, having a new family here. He thought of the day the bishop commissioned him to serve the Longs.

James and Helen were deeply religious. Their choice to build their house just a mile from the new Cathedral was both symbolic and convenient. They attended daily Mass, prayed regularly, and did a great deal of charity work. But as their hearts drew closer to God, it was no longer enough. They only felt the distance more, and yearned for a closer walk.

James built the cell with a window into the Garden Room so the family could receive blessings, reconciliation, and teaching from one who lived his faith heroically. An anchorite: Mr. Long wanted an anchorite.

The bishop turned to Anthony.

Anthony's faith was fervent and deep. Still, he drew in a deep, sharp breath when he heard.

He craved a profound mission that would change him and everyone, indeed the world, around him. He craved the path of the great desert saints—to seek God's will, to commune and worship unceasingly. Instead, he spent his days ministering to the transients and prostitutes of the flophouses and other places of ill repute near the Mississippi River, leaving him, it seemed, little time to pray.

The Bishop offered him what he'd wanted. And yet, to be sealed in a room for the rest of his life—he wondered if he could do it even as he craved such solitude.

The Cathedral itself could benefit from such prayer, the bishop told him. But Mr. Long had requested it. Nobody else in the 19th century would have thought of such an old, old custom.

After praying over it, the bishop agreed to the ancient ritual, rarely used after the 14th century.

In a solemn procession, a dozen brothers, deacons, and priests followed Anthony and the Bishop down the street to the Long mansion. Anthony's heart beat hard, as he walked with the procession, at the thought of the dramatic step he had agreed to. It was for life.

Voices pulled Anthony from his memories. Another realtor repeated the history of the mansion, of James Long the railroad baron. Anthony missed the family. He didn't like hearing them reduced to a history.

"The kids would love this space," said the man. "Room for all of them, with that many bedrooms upstairs. And you'd be really happy in that kitchen. Those stone walls are something else!"

"The family next door has lots of kids, too," the realtor said. "I think you'd be really happy here."

Anthony liked the sound of their voices. He liked the thought of children in the house again. On his kneeler, he closed his eyes, starting to pray they would be the ones.

My Will Be Done.

Anthony sighed. After so many years, he still had not learned.

"Thy will be done," he said.

As the sounds of children's voices came and went, voices he hoped, despite God's gentle warning, would come to stay, Anthony stared at the crucifix, remembering his first sight of it.

The Longs received the procession as they entered the front door. The Bishop made the sign of the cross over the door, the big hall, and the house, sprinkling it with Holy water before James and Helen led the procession down stairs lined with rich mahogany, as beautiful as any main staircase.

The house had every luxury, but this was not on the minds of the party as it moved down the grand basement hall to Anthony's new home, twelve feet square. Inside, Anthony saw a straw mat, a chamber pot, water jug, a chair, cot, and several books. A kneeler faced a Crucifix hung on the wall.

Anthony stared in horror and joy. He felt closer to God already. He felt he was on the verge of a great mission, and he was thankful for this space, this commission, and this desert that was to be his life. He thought of the years of the Long family he would serve and the good they would spread to the outside world.

Thy Will Be Done.

Chapter 1

God wills that we be not carried overly low because of sorrows and temptations that befall us for it has ever been this way before the coming of miracles.

– Revelations of Divine Love, Julian of Norwich

God's Will be Done.

Jacob seemed to hear the words as if from his wall. It wasn't the first time, and it didn't happen often, but it happened again.

"Mama?" He called from his bedroom, down the hall from the kitchen.

"Yes?" She looked up from where she stood by the oven.

"What does it mean for God's will to be done?"

"Come to dinner, Jacob. Wash your hands first."

"But, Mama? What is *God's will*?"

"Can you just get those hands washed!"

"Yes, Mama."

Jacob went to the bathroom across from his room and turned on the faucet. The water ran down from the faucet making a circle near the drain. It went in one direction—like a clock. He turned off the faucet and turned it on again. It happened again—like a clock. Off and on, several times, and again and again—always the same. He forgot about his hands, as the faucet and sink became his lab. Off—on—off—on. Always the same! He thought he caught the water going the other direction once. He turned it on and off really fast, and the water seemed momentarily confused. But every other time—always the same, always clockwise. Minutes passed.

"Jacob? Where are you? Dinner's ready. Are those hands clean?"

"Yes, Mama." He hadn't actually put his hands in the water. He turned off the water, and ran down the hall.

"Daddy?"

"Mmm?"

"You should see what I saw. Every time I turned on the water, it always went down the drain the same way. Always like a clock. I tried a thousand times. Maybe ten thousand. And every time—the same. Always around and around in the same way, like a clock. Have you seen that, Daddy?"

"Mm–hm." His father remained absorbed in his newspaper.

"Daddy?"

His mother slid a plate in front of him and glanced at her phone. Daddy sighed, and set the newspaper down. "Another busy day tomorrow."

Water was circling drains and its story needed to be found out.

God's will.

Jacob lifted his head, listening. *God's will be done.*

Why was the wall saying that?

Anthony was sealed into the cell, the door was shut, and bolted from the outside. The heads were sawed off the bolts so that it would require extensive labor to remove this door. There would be no idle leaving on Anthony's part. The requisite prayers were said: a *Pater Noster, Gloria Patri*, and several *Ave Marias*.

Pater noster qui es in coelis,

sanctificetur nomen tuum;
adveniat regnum tuum,
fiat voluntas tua.

Thy Kingdom come, thy Will be done,
Thy will be done.

As the Bishop finished, Anthony thought, and prayed, "Thy Will Be Done." He listened to the door being sealed. It was finished.

Sealing in represented entombment. It represented death.

He had died to the world, sealed into his tomb. He had died to all but Christ.

His new life in Christ began.

He opened his window, looking into the larger room outside with white walls and floor, tables and windows and a small view through the windows to the outside. With his grate open, he would not be completely shut away from the outside world. On the other side, Mr. and Mrs. Long waited. They greeted him solemnly, "Brother Anthony," and Anthony responded: "In nomine Patris, et Filii, et Spiritus Sancti. Amen." In the Name of the Father, the Son, and the Holy Spirit, Amen.

Anthony prayed over the couple on bended knee.

They arose, shut the window, and left him to his prayers.

That had been long ago. Anthony bowed his head before the cross, praying...praying for those who would move here, praying for his purpose in remaining so long.

After dinner, Jacob went to his room and opened wide his toy castle. It was big—nearly as tall as him! With knights lined up, he rode down the promenade on his horse. Trumpets sounded and banners streamed, as Sir Jacob once more returned from adventure. Ladies waved their kerchiefs, men smiled. Children stopped their play to stare in awe as the great knight passed on his horse. Jacob smiled and waved back to everyone. He paid attention to even the smallest child, and winked when one caught his eye. Flowers fell as if from the sky, and as they sprinkled on his saddle in front of him, he would occasionally pick one up and give it to the lady nearest his side, who blushed, covered her face, and curtsied in response.

In the courtyard of Dun Aoibhneas, he dismounted. Ascending the stairs, he handed parts of his armor and weapons to his squire, Robin. In the Great Hall were more banners and people, and his King at the end of the hall. Methred the Tall sat there, smiling, knowing Jacob's return was good for all.

Jacob joyfully took his seat beside Methred. The court treated his boldness with some exasperation at his familiarity with the king, but more, with pleasure that he was back in the castle, for Methred was happiest when Jacob was home.

They were kindred spirits, ever since that long-ago day Jacob had arrived as a small child at the castle gate, and kindred spirits were not held to the usual rituals of the court. The Queen took Jacob as her own and Jacob and Methred had grown up together, trained, learned, and fought together, beaten each other in foot races and horse races, and been at one another's side since the beginning.

The beginning of what? Of time itself, it seemed. Wizened advisors in the court said they were two halves of the same soul—beyond friends or even brothers—and they were loved by all.

Mothers walked by with daughters in tow, in the most beautiful gowns, their hair beset in bows and flowers. Maidens hoped for proposals. Courtiers and common folk, those with royal blood and those without, all hoped to influence one or both of this pair of great friends, to choose their daughter, sister, or themselves.

Jacob was young—caught in the wonders of his world. He blushed at the attention of young ladies, and their mothers, aunts, grandmothers, handmaids, and everyone else trying to capture his attention, but he was not interested. Methred, recently crowned, was not settled into his office. To choose his queen so soon seemed hasty. Besides, there were adventures to be had, horses to break, streams to swim, mountains to climb, game to hunt, sunshine to outrace—all the whiles and ways of young men who are strong in the world and strong in their sense.

Most importantly—there was a Dragon to be fought.

There was time for courtly pursuits—but that time was not today.

"Jacob? It's time to get ready for bed."

Jacob heard the words like ghostly echoes down an ancient hall. Methred faded. The chair Jacob sat on became his desk chair, and the bright sun of the castle day turned into the twilight of a California evening.

Again his mother called. "Jacob? Are you there? Time for a bath, hon! Let's go!" Jacob parted from Methred and got up to obey his mother.

The bathtub became the setting for more experiments, as Jacob turned on the water. He was fascinated that his experience with the sink was repeated in the tub. Again, the water went down clockwise. Why didn't water just go straight down? Why did it take this curving trip into the drain?

The tub looked simple—just walls and the floor flowing in straight lines right to the drain. Where did the curve come from? He turned the water on. He turned it off. And on. Over and over again. Over and over again the water drained, in the same way, clockwise.

Jacob floated little bits of tissue in the water to see the currents, which always circled the drain before the final plunge into the abyss. He imagined ships he had read about in his books; ships caught in storms in wild and dangerous places, until the doomed crews were caught in the maelstrom of a whirlpool. Sucked in and ever downward, the men set sails and rowed as fast as they could but rarely made it. Narwhals, giant squid, and sea monsters of every shape and form, awaited these poor souls in the center of these giant ocean drains.

Jacob's bits of tissue were the doomed ships, each occupied by a hundred tiny men, sucked in and ever downward, into the abyss. Who knew what awaited them under this tub drain? Jacob shivered at the thought that these creatures were not just of his books, but perhaps inhabited the plumbing in his own home! He had to know!

Jacob stormed out of the bathroom and down the hall. The water in the tub was still flowing, as Jacob shouted, "Mama! Mama!"

In the living room, Jacob's mother looked up, alarmed, from her book and her glass of white wine. "What is it Jacob? What's wrong?"

"Are there giant squid in the plumbing?"

As Mama processed the question, her alarm turned to exasperation, as she noted he was fully dressed. "Jacob! Get back in that bathroom, take your bath, and stop this nonsense! Of course there are no squid in our plumbing!"

"But, Mama! The ships, all those men, the whirlpools—Mama, what's down there then? It's just like in my books!"

"Jacob, I have no idea what you're talking about, but you get in that bathtub right now!"

Jacob turned, not at all confident in his bath. Who knew what doom lurked under the silver cap of the drain, an undefended door to another world where certainly the worst of fates awaited any soul unfortunate enough to descend within it? He thought of the hundreds of tiny souls so recently washed by his own hand down into this doom. Perhaps it was enough to satiate the beasts within. Maybe they wouldn't come for him this time.

He filled the tub, got the job done as quickly as he could, and jumped out, into his pajamas, and ready for bed. He hesitantly opened the drain in the tub, half-expecting a claw from the drain-world to reach for him and try to draw him in. It did not.

As Jacob got into bed, he thought again about what the walls had said earlier in the day. *God's Will Be Done*. What did it mean?

Jacob knew about God—sort of. Mama shouted *God* when she was upset. Or sometimes she said it as she laughed. Jacob stared at the stars on his ceiling—consolations, Mama called them. He wondered what a word meant when you could say it because you were angry *or* because you were happy.

Julio's mom said *Praise God* and Daddy said *Thank God*. And sometimes it came up in discussion between his parents. Jacob tried hard to remember what they'd said. He never remembered, and, really, he hadn't thought about it much even when it came up. But usually Mama seemed irritated when it did. He frowned up at the stars, trying to remember. God had something to do with *church* and Mama didn't like *church*.

So, it was particularly unusual now that he heard this odd phrase. *God's Will Be Done*. As he drifted off to sleep, he wondered why his walls, which typically spoke of deeds in faraway places, had given him this message, at this time.

Chapter 2

In silence and hope will be your strength.

– Ancrene Wisse

It had been coming for some time. Jacob could tell. Sometimes kids just know their parents are up to something, he thought. They look away, they speak in low tones, they try to not make it obvious but it is *so* obvious. And, besides, his parents never talked to him together. Yet, here they were at the big mahogany table in the dining room, not racing to their phones or computers even though they were done eating.

"Jacob?" His mother wore the slim black skirt and white blouse she wore most days to work. Her only concession to walking through the door at the end of the day was to remove the red suit coat and black heels she wore every day.

"Yes, Mama?"

"Your father and I have something to tell you."

Mama never referred to Daddy as "your father." Something was definitely up. A new baby, maybe? His friend Julio had a new baby sister!

At the table, his father nodded and removed his glasses, laying them on the table by a thick red pillar candle.

"You know how your father has been taking lots of business trips?" Mama said.

Jacob nodded eagerly. Maybe he was getting a baby sister on one of those trips? Julio's mom and dad had left for a couple of days, leaving him with his grandmother, and came home with a baby.

"Well, he's been traveling to where he's doing more and more work. So, we thought, rather than have him travel so much, we might just go where he's working. What do you think of that?" His mother smiled broadly.

"You mean, leave this house?" Jacob's heart fluttered in his chest. "But, this is *my* house. I've always been here!"

"Jacob, there are really great houses in Minnesota. In fact, Daddy has been getting very good work there, he's getting a promotion to move there, and we can live in a castle there compared to this small house."

Min-uh-soh-tah, Jacob thought to himself. He had not heard of that. Was Minuh-sohtah even in this country? Was it the same as California? "Mama? Where is Minna-soda?"

"It's pretty far from here. If you get on a plane, it takes four hours to get there."

Jacob had never been on a plane. He had never even imagined being on a plane. He also didn't have a great idea of hours, or time. Time seemed to be one of those things that slipped away on him. He got into trouble often enough for "wasting time," and "running out of time," and other things he didn't really know the meaning of. But, it was clear this "time" concept was important to adults. That he knew. "Mama?"

"Yes, Jacob?"

"What's a plane like?"

She laughed. "You've seen them in your books—like long silver trains with wings, that fly really fast through the sky."

"Like a dragon flies?"

"Well, probably faster than the fastest dragon."

"Dragons can catch anything they want to. Do you think they can catch a plane?"

Jacob's father spoke up. "Jacob, in all of my flying, a dragon has never caught up with one of my planes."

"But it *could* happen."

"Actually, Champ, I think they designed planes to be faster than the fastest dragon."

Jacob doubted that. He wanted to believe his parents, but he *knew* about dragons. There was that time he and Methred rode to face the fiercest dragon of all, the Red Dragon. No matter what they did, that red dragon could shoot back fire, fly faster than they could ride, and do everything to make sure they knew it couldn't be defeated. The dragon won that particular fight, but it would not win the war. Jacob and Methred would see to that.

"Jacob?"

Jacob blinked. The Red Dragon faded away and his mother stared at him. Her eyebrows dipped down over her green eyes as if she'd spoken several times. "Yes, Mama?" he said.

"We'll be moving to Minnesota in two months. We've put this house up for sale, and we found a really nice one in Minnesota. In June, you'll be done with school, and you can start first grade in St. Paul."

Jacob had spent his life in the Montessori here, from before his earliest memories through pre-school and kindergarten. He had friends here. Also, he had seen how new kids got treated. They weren't invited to sit at anyone's table, no one picked them for teams at gym. Usually one of his friends would eventually go up to the new kid and become friends. Sometimes it was because they lived nearby, or their parents knew each other, or something. He didn't want to be the new kid—the kid who no one picked, ate lunch with, or talked to.

"Mama?"

"Yes, Jacob?"

"What if I don't make friends at the new school?"

"Oh, sweetie, you'll make friends."

He hated being called "sweetie." It made him feel weird.

"St. Paul is a big city, and there are lots of people there. I bet you'll have new friends in no time. We even saw a boy about your age living right next to the house we bought."

So they weren't really asking what he thought. They'd already bought the house.

He kicked his legs back and forth a few times before asking softly, "What's the house like?"

"It's pretty amazing," Daddy said.

"It was built by a railroad baron in the early nineteenth century," Mama said.

"What's a baron? What's a nine-teeth sentry?"

"A baron is a very rich man and the early nineteenth century was more than a hundred years ago."

"So the house is really old?" Jacob asked.

Daddy nodded. "They don't build them like that anymore. We're very lucky!"

"What if there's a ghost?" Jacob's forehead wrinkled. "Old houses have ghosts."

"Who told you that?" Mama said it in her irritated voice.

"Julio."

"Well, Julio's family believes some things that just aren't true." Mama got up, taking her plate and Daddy's in one hand, and the pan of braised talapia in the other and heading to the kitchen.

"What *is* a ghost?" Jacob asked when she was gone.

Daddy leaned forward, his eyes bright like they got when he was excited. He lowered his voice. "Nobody knows for sure, but *I* think...they're the spirits of people don't realize they're dead. So they stay where they were, thinking they're still alive."

Jacob frowned a little.

Daddy patted his hand. "It's a great house. You're going to love it. And there are no ghosts."

Jacob liked Rancho Bernardo. There were nice houses. San Diego was close. There were mountains to bike in and visit. And a school he liked, where he knew the other kids.

"Can we bring Julio?" he asked. "He's my best friend. Can we bring him?"

Mama came back into the dining room at that moment, taking Jacob's plate. "No, dear, he'll need to stay here with his own parents. To bed, young man."

Jacob got up from the table and headed to his room.

Behind him, he heard them murmuring, "Well, I think that went well..." and more discussion in hushed tones he couldn't hear.

As Jacob went back to his room and closed the door, the sound was unmistakable. *God's Will Be Done.*

There it was again! Like a low rumble from the wall, the voice spoke as if from outside, and yet inside. Jacob looked hard at the wall.

It fell silent, holding its secrets.

Jacob lay on his bed. The room was dark, except for the lights shining outside. The window was open on this nice night in spring, and a slight breeze rustled the curtains. The smell of many wonderful flowers and plants came in through the window. The sprinkler systems around the neighborhood turned on, filling the night with the sound of misting water and sprinkler heads creaking and squeaking as they turned. Jacob heard water bounce off the fronds of a broad-leafed plant, and the trunk of a palm tree, as the sprinkler went one way and then the other. It was a peaceful sound that reminded him of the burble of the river outside Dun Aoibhneas.

Beautiful Dun Aoibhneas with its high stone walls!

"Jacob! How goes the struggle, my good and finest knight?"

"Methred! Indeed, it goes well. I am without injury from our latest skirmish with the Red Dragon, and we think we may be able to advance upon him soon."

"Excellent! This menace must be brought to heel, Sir Jacob! Let no one in this court think otherwise! The kingdom itself is threatened by this infernal creature!"

Those in the court this fine afternoon bowed, all eyes on Jacob, as he reported from the field.

Courts often had intrigue. But not Dun Aoibhneas, not tonight. Jacob was an accomplished knight and a popular one, and all wished him well. After all, the king, the kingdom, and the people themselves, all benefited from Jacob's campaigns.

"Thy Will Be Done."

In his cell, on his knees before the Crucifix, Anthony repeated the words again to himself, as he so often did. "God's Will Be Done." His prayer was simple, yet it was all he desired. To be one with God. To know God's will entirely and perfectly, to desire nothing but to follow Him and know Him. To contemplate it, live it—eat, sleep, and drink it. To need nothing else.

To *be* God's will—in the lives of others. To make life better for God's children; perhaps to open to God's children, in some ways, the doors to the beautiful Interior Mansions.

He had done this for James and Helen, for their children—and finally their grandchildren. And in between, he devoted himself to prayer, to the visions God granted him, that carried him through days, through weeks...or longer.

He would emerge from visions to Ted Long, the grandson, knocking at his window.

But the Longs were—well, long gone, Anthony thought ruefully. They had lived into their 80s, doing great good for others. Was it not enough? Was his prayer making the world better for the people God loved, as he knelt here alone, day after day, month after month?

He loved being able to devote his days to prayer, to adoration, to Love and contemplation of God. But sometimes he got bored. Lonely. With the last of the Longs having left, his days had changed. What of this confusion, this doubt? Why would he, of all followers of Christ, ever doubt? This could be what he reaped for his doubt—more time. Maybe this was why his commission continued? More and more time, with less and less to show for it—because was he really doing any good for the world, enclosed in his cell, praying endlessly?

But truthfully, he reminded himself, he had work to do here. Had he not, God would have called him home. A new family was moving in. They would be like the Longs, he was sure: A family who loved God, who sought prayer and enlightenment. He was sure it would be the family who spoke of space for their many children—a family, perhaps, like the Lovards next door, with parents and children who longed to know God more deeply.

He bowed his head in thanks for the family he anticipated.

God's Will Be Done.

Chapter 3

"Throw out Fear, our enemy," says Caution, "there is no room in this house for both of them, for where the messenger of Joy is, and true Love of eternal Life, Fear is put to flight."

– Sawles Warde

Jacob climbed from his father's Mercedes, pulling his backpack with his books onto his back and dragging his little blue suitcase out onto the sidewalk beside him. He'd stayed with his grandmother for two days while his parents came ahead to direct the packers and start setting the new house to rights. Grandma had put him on a plane this morning in the care of a thin woman in a skirt and heels like Mama's. He'd read his books about ships and stars and looked at the clouds soaring beneath him, watching for dragons—which thankfully there were none—and Mama and Daddy had met him as he got off the plane.

He stared up, now, at the big stone house on the hill. It was enormous —six or seven of his little house in Rancho Bernardo could fit inside it he was sure—and so red.

A huge church—Mama called it a *cathedral*—was just down the street. Mama spoke of it as if it was important—as if *they* were important for living so close to it. Jacob didn't understand why. His mother didn't care for church. "That's for weak people too afraid to live life on their own," she'd once said. So shouldn't she be unhappy to have a *cathedral* so close?

Jacob imagined a house full of people too weak to carry their own suitcases, as he had carried his through the airport; barely strong enough to climb out of bed and crawl to the table, and too weak to lift their spoons to their mouths to eat.

He wondered why they were so weak. He would have to ask Daddy what made people strong. Then maybe he could help those people.

"Jacob?" His father's voice cut through his thoughts as if he'd spoken more than once.

Jacob looked up. "Yes, Daddy?"

"Your mother asked what you think."

It was *big,* Jacob thought, with a wide front and huge turrets just like a castle that rose two stories and a window looking down from way up on the third floor and his parents said there was a basement, too, big enough for him to ride his bike in.

"Quite the cellar," Mama had said, and they'd both laughed.

It wasn't so big as Methred's castle—but then a hundred people lived in Methred's castle. Here, there would be only the three of them.

Without waiting for an answer, his mother said, "Summit Hill is *the* place to be. You'll meet the right people here—people who have money and make things happen. Who open doors to you in the future when you become a lawyer like your father. There's a supreme court judge and a famous author."

"Will I get lost inside?" Jacob asked.

His mother laughed. "Not for long."

It didn't reassure him. He remembered wandering the halls of Methred's castle when he had been very young. He'd gotten lost in the twisting halls and a servant girl had to lead him back to the great hall.

"Let's go, Champ," his father said. "You're gonna love this. You love stories of castles, after all, and this even has ruins in the back!"

"Ruins?" Jacob asked.

His father grabbed his hand, the one that wasn't holding his blue suitcase, leading him swiftly up the short sidewalk and up the stairs. The suitcase rattled behind on its wheels, bumping up the stairs and onto a very wide, red stone front porch with high walls looking back out to the world. At their side, his mother pulled a key from her purse and opened the front door.

"What are ruins?" Jacob asked.

"When a castle or a cathedral has fallen down," his father answered. "When just some of the stone walls are left."

His mother pushed open the door. At the same time, an image flashed before Jacob's eyes of Dun Aoibhneas—the roof gone, the floors gone— only stark stone walls reaching for the sky with empty eyes where glass had once filled the windows. His heart pounded faster.

"Why would a castle fall down?" he demanded. "What happened to the people inside?"

"Richard, why do you bring these things up?" his mother demanded. "You know how he is. Jacob, come inside and see your new house! Nothing's happened to anyone." She flung the door wide and Jacob felt dizzy for a second, staring at the vast hall inside. It was big and square— not an entry but an entire room with a fireplace almost as big as those in Methred's great hall. A marble floor! A ceiling with designs on it. A massive staircase and heavy wooden paneled doors that slid right into the walls. Hundreds of boxes filled the room to the right. At the far end of the big hall, sunlight poured through the thick glass of two wide doors.

"Those go to the back veranda and the yard," Mama said, seeing the direction of his gaze.

"Want me to show you around?" his father asked.

Jacob nodded eagerly. His father was usually too busy for such things —for anything. Being a lawyer, Jacob knew, took a lot of time. He didn't really know, beyond that, what it meant to be a lawyer. Except you made lots of money.

"Richard, we have a lot of work to do," Mama said. "I'm sure Jacob will have fun running around and exploring on his own."

"Yes, Faith." His dad sighed, looking at the walls of boxes piled high. "Okay, Champ. Go look around. Pick what bedroom you want. There's one in the basement—"

"Our root cellar," Mama said, and laughed as she started to rip open a box.

"I'm guessing you don't want that," Daddy said, "and a few on the second floor and a couple in the attic. There's a ballroom up there, too."

"Like the ball pit at Fun Land!" For the first time, Jacob thought this might not be so bad after all, envisioning a thousand brightly colored balls to roll and jump in.

His father laughed. "Not that kind of ball."

"They held dances there." Mama worked at the tape holding a box together, her back to him.

Jacob waited, hoping his father would change his mind. The place was huge.

"Richard." His mother's voice came out sharply. "These boxes aren't going to unpack themselves. I have to meet my new supervisor tomorrow and I don't want to live like this for the next six months."

Jacob turned to wander through the house.

It was big—but it wasn't so hard to find his way around as he'd feared. It helped, of course, that he'd learned to navigate Methred's castle, quickly understanding that it was just a big square. This house wasn't so different. The kitchen was a huge room with stone walls, to the left of the big fireplace room while the living room where his parents worked at the boxes was to its right. Upstairs, all the bedrooms flowed back into the hallway where a large dark bannister looked down into the rooms below and ran down the side of broad stairs.

The second floor hall ran between the railing overlooking the big entry square below and a huge bookcase on the wall. In the days Jacob had stayed at Grandma's, Daddy had already filled most of the shelves with his law books and journals and set up his new office at the top of the stairs, just off to the right. It was one of the tower rooms. Its big, curving window had a big, curving window seat with thick cushions. Jacob jumped up, kneeling on them with his hands pressed to the tall windows to see the world below: a thin woman running with a big, black dog, an older boy with a backpack, and cars driving past.

Jacob hopped off the cushion and wandered in and out of the bedrooms, with piles of boxes, some already with curtains and beds with sheets and pictures on the walls—all the things from their house in California. Two rooms had fireplaces. His parents' bed stood in front of the big curving windows on the second floor of another tower room at the back of the house. Boxes stood piled up against the walls.

Jacob crossed back over the hall to another bedroom—more bowed windows, his own bed in pieces on the floor. Another hall led to a long room on the side of the house. It had a stone floor and three walls full of windows. On the long wall, three windows each had big stone arches over them—a big window in the middle between two slightly smaller ones. He pressed his nose to the screen, looking down into the yard of the house next door. A girl stood on the roof of the porch. She glanced at him, waved, and leapt off. Jacob gasped.

Then he saw that she landed on a trampoline below and bounced— one, two, three times, laughing in glee.

Four boys ran around the yard. One of them scrambled up onto the trampoline and began bouncing, too, grinning and waving at Jacob every time he flew up in the air.

Jacob ducked away. He didn't know how to make new friends. He'd always had his friends in his neighborhood and school. Always!

In his cell below, Anthony roused from an intense vision of God on His throne, a place of singing and joy. The last thing he remembered was the sound of many feet above, dragging box after box, and voices calling to one another.

With so many boxes, it must be so many children, he'd thought, and returned to his prayers, grateful to God.

Now, emerging from a vision, the room felt dark and cold—not so much because it was dark but because it lacked the light of God he had just experienced. Still, he came back to his cell with an even greater conviction that God had left him here, for so many years, because he still had work to do. He looked forward to meeting the family above. He heard muffled voices upstairs and the sound of children's laughter outside. He couldn't wait to meet them. He wondered how many there were. Five? Seven? More?

Jacob raced through the myriad of rooms, down the wide, mahogany hall, and down the broad stairs. "I found my room!" he shouted. Excitement welled in him. It was the best room ever with lots of space to fly around like a dragon and set up his big castle and all his armies and horses and a stone floor just like in Methred's castle.

"Jacob, not quite so loud." Mama pressed two fingers to her temple.

"I'm sorry, Mama."

Moments later, he stood with his parents in the wonderful room, full of windows and sunlight.

Mama frowned. "Jacob, this isn't a bedroom. It's a sun room."

"*I'm* a son!" Jacob said. It *was* a great room for boys, he thought.

Daddy laughed.

"Not that kind of son," Mama said. "It's not a *bed*room."

"But we *can* put my bed in it," Jacob said. "Look—I can put all my toys and bookshelves there under all the windows."

"But there's no closet," Mama said.

"Well there's a bedroom just across the hall," Daddy said. "We could put his clothes there. It's not like we're over-crowded in here."

"It's going to be awfully cold in the winter." Mama shook her head. "I'm sorry, Jacob, this won't do. You can have the bedroom across the hall."

Jacob's face fell. "But you said…."

Daddy put a hand on his shoulder, giving him a quick shake of the head as Mama turned to go. "Faith."

She turned, waiting.

"We did say he could pick out his own bedroom."

"We said he could pick out a *bed* room—not just pick any old room to camp out in."

"His bed is easy enough to move," Daddy said. "This *is* a great room for his toys and book shelves, so let's just move all of that in here and let him have his bed here for the summer and when the weather gets cold we'll just move his bed."

"It's not a *bed* room," Mama insisted.

"Look, let's just let him sleep here for a night or two and then we can sort this out, okay? Then he can spend today setting up his toys and leave us to our work."

Mama rolled her eyes and lifted her chin, staring at the ceiling in annoyance. Jacob glanced up at it. It had wood paneling, like some of the walls, and a fancy chandelier.

"All *right*," Mama said. "But only so I can get back to work."

Daddy winked at Jacob as Mama's footsteps disappeared down the mahogany hall. "Let's go get your bed, Buddy!"

Jacob smiled.

The voices drifted to Anthony's ears, pulling him from his reading of *The Ancrene Wisse* and his contemplation of the Agony in the Garden.

"Richard," said a woman's voice, "I'm disappointed you didn't back me on the bedroom. That is *not* a proper bedroom and it would have been a beautiful place to have teas."

"Who are you going to have tea with?" the man asked.

"When I join the parents' group at the Academy…."

"He hasn't been accepted…."

"But he will be and I'll be on committees and it would have been lovely to…."

"But we have half a dozen other rooms just as beautiful and a sun room just like it right below that room."

Their voices drifted away, hers peevish, toward the big sunny room.

Anthony bowed his head in disappointment. This was not the family he had hoped for. His heart told him the woman behind this voice would not want to talk to him. He dropped to his knees on his kneeler.

Why, God? He thought. *Why did You bring a family here who doesn't want me?*

My will be done.

He heard the words audibly and he swore he felt, in his mind's eye, a gentle, humorous smile behind the words, before the couple's voices approached again.

This time, the woman was excited. "M.M. Love! A signed copy!"

"He must have known the Longs," said the man. There was a silence before he said, "I didn't know he wrote non-fiction."

"It's about some of the research he did for his books—supposedly historical accounts of fantastical events."

"Well, there *is* more to this world than we know of," said the man. Their voices were right outside the Garden Room.

The woman laughed. "It's nonsense of course. The medieval mind was a very superstitious mind. All the same—his books are being made into movies. He can't be very far from us. I want to have a joint birthday party, house-warming party. It would be great to invite him." Her voice decrescendoed down the hall. "We'll have to figure out where he lives, look for a chance to introduce ourselves. That mustache is distinctive— shouldn't be hard to spot."

Their footsteps sounded up the stairs and faded away.

The boy will be coming soon.

These were not audible words. They were not even words fully formed in his mind. They were a mere impression. But Anthony had learned to trust such impressions. *Jacob.*

Thy will be done, Anthony replied. He prayed for Jacob.

Chapter 4

Come now, thou poor child of man, turn awhile from thy business, hide thyself for a little time from restless thoughts, cast away thy troublesome cares, put aside thy wearisome distractions. Give thyself a little leisure to converse with God.

– Proslogion by St. Anselm

With his bed set up in the far corner of the room, Jacob happily scrambled over it, tugging and pulling at his sheets as Mama had taught him to do. While Daddy moved his shelves in—long, low cubbies that held books and toys—Jacob ran through the big house eagerly seeking boxes with his name on them. He could read *Jacob* and *toys* and *books* and quite a lot more. He could read entire books by himself.

He pushed some of the cubbies under the windows and others against the stone wall opposite the three windows. He found the box that said *castle* in one of the bedrooms and joyfully hefted and dragged it down the hall to his new room.

Soon his castle stood grandly at one end of his room, with its flags carefully placed back on the parapets and its many knights lined up on the castle walls or riding out across the drawbridge.

He took his bath after dinner and climbed into bed, happy in his freshly-made bed pushed up beneath the smaller arch on the long wall. The open window let in cool night air.

My will be done.

The words brushed gently on Jacob's mind. Jacob sat up, listening intently. Why was the same voice here in this house? He listened a long time—but the voice didn't speak again.

He laid back on his pillow and stared up at the consolation chart Mama had told Daddy to fix to the wooden ceiling, covering almost half the room and glowing softly in the dark, showing all the stars and how they made people and animals in the sky. He fell asleep, drifting back to Dun Aoibhneas and a ball in the great hall and his talks long into the night with Methred about how to confront the Red Dragon.

Over the next week Jacob meticulously set his books in the order he liked them, with all the books about outer space together with their big, bright pictures of stars and planets, and all his books about castles and knights together, and his books about creatures in the sea together and more. He arranged his toys carefully and hung his dress shirts and suit coats in the closet in the other room—one bar was low so he could reach it—and folded his pants and shirts neatly, as Mama liked them to be, and put them in the dresser. In between putting away, he explored the house. He especially liked the big kitchen with its stone walls—like the stone outside except it was inside—and the strange narrow room off the kitchen with counters and shelves. A *butt-ler's pantry,* Mama said. All old houses had them, because they'd been built in the days when families all had butt-lers.

Jacob thought of the goat the day his kindergarten class went to the petting zoo. It had tried to butt him and had to be led away and put in the barn. He was glad they wouldn't have a butt-ler. It seemed like something Mama wouldn't want, anyway. So he didn't understand why she spoke of a butt-ler pantry like it was something to be proud of.

It must be like being proud of living near a cathedral full of weak people, Jacob thought. Some things about adults he just didn't understand.

Butt-ler. Ant-ler. He wondered if ants had antlers.

Jacob explored the 'ball room' far up on top of the house. Though his parents had warned him there were no balls he was still disappointed. He'd hoped they were wrong. No baseballs, no golf balls, no colorful balls like the pits at the play place, no basketballs.

He ran his cars and trains along the *veranda* that stretched along the back of the house, looking over an iron gate and down broad red stone stairs to a red stone fountain in the back yard and a view that stretched right off the end of the yard which seemed to fall to the city spread below and a big bridge that crossed a river his mother called *Miss Sippy*. At night in his bed, he thought who Miss Sippy might be and what she might look like.

Jacob went to his father's new office every day, while Daddy unpacked or worked on his computer, to sit on the big cushions and look out to the world below, to people coming and going.

On the day Mama was going to take him to his new school, the day she told him to put on his dress shirt and suit coat, a woman carried a little boy, younger than Jacob, out of the house next door, to a big van. A couple of kids waved to them from the front door as the van pulled away. Then they looked up at him and smiled and waved. Jacob wanted to wave. But he was afraid.

He jumped off the window seat and ran from the room, down the big, wide staircase, all the way down to the basement—or the cellar as his mother called it. She laughed every time she said it.

There he stopped in surprise. Cellars, he thought, were dark and dreary like the dungeons of Dun Aoibhneas. It was why he'd stayed out of the basement.

But this! This looked like the country club his father took them to in California. Sconces on the walls pooled soft light on dark elegant paneling. A deep crimson runner unfurled down the hall. Jacob dropped to his knees, touching the floor that showed on either side of the carpet. It was of beautiful stone tiles. He climbed to his feet, looking around. There was a large room at the far end of the basement.

He moved slowly down the long hall, looking up in wonder at paneling worthy of Methred's castle, to the crown molding at the top. Several doors lined the hall. He dared not look in them, lest he find dragons guarding treasure. He had enough dragons to deal with at Dun Aoibhneas! He didn't need to find any here!

He reached the large room at the end. Its walls were white-washed cement. White iron racks ran around the walls, holding lush, green plants. A bed stood in the center. Mama had said the previous owners would leave some things. Jacob studied the room closely. It had wide, narrow windows at the tops of the walls that spilled in tons of sunshine. One of them was open and he could hear the children next door laughing.

He crept closer to the bed. It had an old-fashioned white iron frame and a heavy quilt that seemed to have come from long ago.

Thy will be done.

Jacob spun! His eyes wide, he scanned the room again. It was empty.

Behind the greenery, he suddenly realized there was a stair disappearing into the wall. It looked much like the stairs in Methred's castle—like the one behind the throne that almost no one knew about. Jacob inched up to it, peering in and up. He could hear his mother's voice somewhere above, directing his father to put the china away while she attended a work meeting online—it was vitally important—and be sure to start sorting out *those tools of his* in the garage. "We don't have much room out there," she said. "It'll have to be well-organized to leave space for the car."

Jacob trod quietly up the secret stairs. They turned inside the wall, taking him to a narrow opening from which he could see the grand living room and his father working.

Unwrapping the good china, Daddy said, "I thought I'd take Jacob out to see the ruins."

"We have plenty of time for that later." His mother called back over her shoulder as she headed to the room that was now her office, "We've been here nine days already and we're still not unpacked. It has to get done."

"Fifteen minutes."

Mama shook her head. "Besides, I have the appointment with Jacob at his new school. This unpacking just has to get done."

Jacob stood quietly by the wall.

"Yes, true." His father stared after his mother, shook his head, and continued his work.

Jacob crept down the stairs, back to the sunny basement room. He walked around, studying the plants that thrived there, and running a hand over the old quilt. It had four large panels. The upper right showed two black horses facing each other from either side of a tree. The lower left showed one proud black stallion. The upper left had a white dog or fox in the center of a laurel wreath while its opposite square showed a white horse and a white dog looking at each other in front of a big white two-story house beside a tree.

His mother wouldn't like it. She would certainly replace it with something bright and new. That made Jacob sad. He wondered who had made it. He touched the big white farmhouse—he knew it was a farmhouse, somehow—what else could it be? Was it the house of whoever made the quilt? Was that their beloved dog memorialized in the bed cover?

Had those horses existed? He stared into the tiny black knots of thread that made their eyes.

Pepper. Lee.

Jacob smiled. "Hi, Pepper. Hi, Lee. You should come to Methred's castle with me. Methred could use a fine pair of horses like you." He thought maybe he'd take the quilt—hide it in his room before Mama saw it and threw it out.

Barkee! Jacob's smile grew, as his eyes turned to the white dog. He almost imagined it wagged its tail. "You, too," he said. "Did your boy get old?" It had to have been a boy, probably his own age, who named the dog Barkee.

Thy will be done.

Jacob spun. With the horses and the dog reassuring him—he felt they were telling him, *It's okay, he's our friend!* – Jacob ran into the hall. On his right, a broad pair of doors with dozens of small glass panes opened into a bright, sunny room. Like the big room, its windows were set high, but if he stood on tiptoe, way back, he could see the wide lawn, above, and the big stone fountain much like that in Methred's courtyard, and gardens full of colorful flowers. A small brown door with a window showed a short flight of stairs leading up to the yard.

The room itself held what seemed to be hundreds more green plants—almost a jungle! They sat on low tables by the window, on a tall granite-topped table in the middle of the room, on shelves on the walls! Jacob laughed out loud at the life in the room. He flung his arms out, spinning in a circle and dancing around the big table, with plants and lush greenery on either side and sunlight pouring in the window. How could a basement room have windows to the outside?

"They are beautiful, aren't they?"

Jacob stopped as quickly as he'd started.

"He said you'd be coming."

Jacob turned slowly. This side of the room had the same dark wood paneling as the hall. Only now—he saw the inset in the paneling. A small *hiss* sounded, and a panel slid, exposing a large window with bars across it.

Jacob took a step closer.

A man sat inside, smiling out at him. "You *are* Jacob, aren't you?" he said.

Jacob gasped. Then he quickly said, "Pepper and Lee and Barkee said you're their friend. They said not to be scared of you."

The man beamed. "They were good horses. And Barkee was a fine dog."

Jacob could see, as his eyes adjusted to the dim light inside the cell, that the man was bald on the top of his head. He seemed a little older than Daddy, but not much. He wore a heavy brown robe with a cowl around his shoulders.

"Are you a Franciscan?" Jacob asked. The Franciscans worked and prayed at Methred's castle.

"I am indeed! My name is Anthony. I'm pleased to meet you."

Jacob cocked his head. "Why are you in our walls?"

"I'm an anchorite."

"What's an ank-rite?"

The man in the wall smiled. "Someone who prays."

"But why are you praying in our *walls*?"

"Mr. and Mrs. Long asked me to when they lived here."

"Didn't they die a hundred years ago?"

Anthony tilted his head, frowning. "Maybe not quite so long as that. They lived to be quite old—well into the 1930s."

"But why are you still here?"

"Because no one has told me to leave. I live in my hermitage here and pray for the families in this house as I strive to become a saint."

Before Jacob could ask what a saint was, he heard his mother's voice coming from the stairs. "Jacob! Jacob, where are you? It's time to go visit your new school!"

"I'll be back!" Jacob mounted his ebony horse, Pepper, and with Barkee racing at his side, galloped up the stairs, almost crashing into his mother. "Mama!" he cried, "there's a man in our walls down there!"

"What took you so long?" she asked.

"Mama, there's a…."

"I heard you," she said. "Stop this nonsense. You know there are no men in the walls just like there's no Methelred."

"Methred."

She squatted down, perched carefully on her heels in her slim black skirt, and took his hands in hers. "Jacob, you really are getting too old to have imaginary friends. You're going into first grade." She studied his hair with a sharp eye and smoothed it down, then held out his suit coat for him.

"But Mama, it's true," Jacob said as he struggled into the sleeves. "He said he's trying to be a saint. We have a saint in our cellar!"

He didn't know what a saint was, but he liked the sound of it.

Mama clipped his tie onto his shirt collar, then rose in one fluid motion to her elegant height above him. "Jacob, there is absolutely no one there," she said as she turned to reach for the car keys. "Now don't stray off the sidewalk and get dirt on your shoes or pants. This is the very best school in the Twin Cities. They've done us a huge favor in considering you ahead of some of the other children on the waiting list. You need to present a good image to Miss Marple."

"He said Mr. and Mrs. Long asked him in. They died in the 1930s when they were in their 80s."

Mama stopped.

She turned slowly, looking down at him. "How do you know about the previous owners?"

Jacob's lower lip trembled just for a second as he stared at his mother in surprise. "I just told you. Anthony told me."

Mama spun and marched, her heels *click-clacking* on the parquet floor. "Richard?" Raising her voice she called into the living room. "Richard, did you tell Jacob about the Longs?"

Daddy stuck his head out around a pile of boxes that reached up to the ceiling. "No, Faith." He looked surprised. "Why in the world would I be talking about the Longs?"

Mama gave a little sniff, and *click-clacked* back to Jacob, taking his hand and leading him out the front door onto the broad red stone porch. "You need to stop the fanciful stories. Certainly do not tell Miss Marple these things."

Thy will be done.

Jacob heard the words in his head and he felt he could see Anthony smiling. He felt Pepper prancing along beside him. He would make a fine steed at Dun Aoibhneas. He beamed up at his mother. "Yes, Mama!"

He couldn't wait to run down to the basement and talk to Anthony again.

Chapter 5

As Job says, those who dig for a hoard of gold, the closer they get to it, the more ardent gladness of heart makes them, and the keener to dig and delve deeper and deeper until they find it. Your heart is not on earth, so you need not delve downward….What is that delving? Eager, seeking thought: where it is, what it is; how it can be found. This is the delving: to be busily and eagerly always about it, with a constant yearning, with the heat of a hungry heart….

– Ancrene Wisse

Jacob swung his feet under his chair at dinner.

Daddy dished the carry-out sushi onto plates at the big, long table—a table Jacob thought would look good in the great hall of Dun Aoibhneas. It didn't even fill the huge dining room with the tin ceiling with circles all over it.

Mama removed her red suit coat, hanging it carefully over the back of her chair. She poured sake for herself and Daddy and milk for Jacob, and sank into her seat.

"Can't I have sock-E?" Jacob asked.

Dad laughed. "You're a little under age."

"Ale, then?"

"Jacob, *please.*" Mama pushed a hand through her dark hair.

"I always have ale with Methred."

Mama sighed. "You need to stop talking about Methelred. He's not real."

"His name is Methred."

Mama picked up her chopsticks, but instead of eating, said to Daddy, "He embarrassed me in front of Miss Marple. He started talking about Methelred and Du' Novnis."

Daddy picked up a piece of sushi between two black chopsticks, dipping it in soy and wasabi. "I'm sure Miss Marple saw that he's imaginative and knows quite a lot for his age."

Jacob only half heard his father's words as he studied the piece of fish on top of his sushi.

"What is this, Mama?" He picked it off the top of the rice with his fingers.

"Jacob!" She sounded horrified. "Use chop sticks."

"Let him use a fork," Daddy said.

Mama huffed. "He has to learn to use them sooner or later. It'll be important in the business world."

Jacob looked up at her, still swinging his feet. "I'm sorry, Mama." He took the chop sticks she offered and tried to work them into his fingers. They kept slipping.

"Use a fork, Jacob," Daddy said. "We'll work on the chop sticks tomorrow. Faith, he has plenty of time to learn. He's only five."

"Yes, and in a few months he'll be six and the next thing you know, he'll be in high school and off to college. We can't put things off."

"But Mama, what is this on top of the rice?"

"Tuna," she said shortly, and took a deep sip of her sake. "Richard, I don't know what to do with him."

"I know it's last name!" Jacob announced excitedly.

"He's fine," Daddy answered.

Jacob pulled at his father's sleeve. "Daddy, I know Tuna's last name!"

"He may be rejected by the Academy because of this!"

"But Mama, I'm smart and I know a lot! I know all about castles and knights and consolations in the sky and I know Tuna's last name!"

"Tuna does not have a last name," she said. "It's a fish." At that moment, her phone beeped. She let out a bad word—just one of the smaller bad words.

Jacob tilted his head, watching as she answered her phone. Methred didn't allow bad words in Dun Aoibhneas. He believed in courtly manners.

"Yes, Dan," Mama said. Dan was her business partner. "This proposal isn't due until Wednesday." She listened before saying, "But he's wrong about that. I told him at least five times…."

Through his prayers, Anthony heard a door open and close, far above. The sound pulled him from a vision of Christ standing beside young Jacob, warding off a red dragon with an upraised shepherd's staff. He opened his eyes to the candlelit cell, listening to the voice of irritation.

What is it You want, Father? He asked silently. *What can I possibly do from here.*

Even as he asked the question, he knew the answer:

Pray, my child.

Hadn't he prayed here for years? And hadn't he always seen the answers to his prayers?

For whom do I pray, Father? The boy? His mother?

The image of the red dragon flashed into his mind again. Its eyes were a brilliant jade green. It's stomach rumbled as if hungry and it salivated. It was always hungry, Anthony understood.

But hungry for what?

He pondered the hungers of the world. Man should hunger for that which lasts all eternity, and satisfies eternally—God. But Man, Anthony thought, was not rational. Instead of hungering for peace, justice, goodness, and love, Man hungered for power, renown, money, fame, prestige.

He had talked many an evening as James Long sat by the grate, about the things men spent their lives seeking.

"I spent my early years seeking money." Mr. Long sat outside the cell, his head bowed. He waved a hand around the room full of plants, indicating the whole, the expensive and luxurious house with its towers and mahogany paneling and grand staircase and ornate fireplaces and more, and gave a sad chuckle. "I succeeded. But every time I reached what I thought would make me happy—I wasn't."

They had talked late into the night about Jame's childhood and all that *his* father had hungered for, about why James himself hungered so for money.

Anthony thought about the family above. He had prayed often, in the silent years since the Longs had moved on—prayed for the souls of the Longs, of their elderly daughter and the not-nearly-so-elderly grandsons who, even until the house sold, had come to sit or kneel outside his grate, talking to him, sometimes late into the night as their father and grandfather had, seeking wisdom, seeking confession, absolution.

They didn't know they sought wisdom or absolution, Anthony thought. But why else does one speak to an anchorite? They called it *counseling*. They looked for affirmation—or a new direction. They spoke sometimes of miracles after asking for his prayers—of a job opening at just the right time, of meeting just the right person, the price of a house dropping.

In the early years, they'd called it *coincidence*.

As the years rolled on, they spoke of insights and seeing more clearly how they needed God, of a growing hunger for Him.

What were these few souls, Anthony wondered? Out in the world, might he not work to bring thousands to Christ and the joy He offered?

My will be done.

The words were strong and clear, as if etched on his mind, as if spoken, but from far away. Anthony remembered the sin of Pride and prayed for forgiveness.

"Hey, Bud," Daddy said, as Mama talked on the phone, and Jacob turned back to him. "How did you like the Academy?"

"Miss Marple is nice," Jacob said.

"What about the classrooms?"

"What if I don't make friends?" Jacob asked.

His mother continued to argue with Dan.

"Hey, Bud, you'll be fine," Daddy said. "All you have to do...." His phone beeped. "Give me a second," he said, and looked at the phone. He glanced back at Jacob. "Sorry, I have to deal with this. Big client. I'm still getting up to speed."

When Mama turned her back, Jacob picked up the sushi with his fingers and took a bite. "That's why fish have scales," he said. "Tuna. Tuna." He smiled at his mother. She frowned at him, as Dan reeled off a long string of words that came over the phone.

"No, Dan," she said, turning away again. "That won't do."

By the time she hung up, Jacob had finished eating his sushi with his fingers. He propped the chopsticks in his hands.

She smiled at him. "Very good, Jacob."

Jacob smiled back.

His father set down his phone, too. "Work email," he said. "I had to get an answer to Ben immediately."

"Piano!" Jacob announced to his parents. "Fish like music."

Mama pushed a hand through her hair. "Fish don't know anything about music. Why are you asking nonsensical questions, Jacob?"

"Fish have scales and music has scales."

Daddy chuckled. Jacob wasn't sure why that was funny.

"His last name is Piano," Jacob said.

"Whose last name?" Mama asked.

"Tuna." Jacob swung his legs beneath his chair. "Tuna Piano and he has scales."

Mama rolled her eyes. "I'm too tired for this." She pushed her chair back. "Richard, I'm going to have to ask you to clean up tonight. I have to call Miss Marple and see what I can do to make sure Jacob gets in. Jacob, you go up and take your bath."

"But I want to go see…"

"Bath," Mama said.

Jacob slid off his chair and headed across the big vestibule with the big fireplace to the stairs, disappointed. He wanted to see Anthony.

Through the years of the empty house, Anthony had prayed for the right family to move here—a family that needed him. He had heard Faith's voice the two times she and Richard had come through looking at the house. He had heard many voices pass through these walls, of potential buyers. Some, he had hoped—even dared pray—would move here. Some of the women reminded him of Helen Long, of her kindness, her devotion, her desire to do good in the world, her *faith.*

Faith—he had specifically prayed—would *not* move here. Her voice carried through the walls, even from above, finding fault, speaking over her husband, correcting the realtor, demanding.

Thy will be done, Anthony had prayed over and over.

He sank back to his knees on his kneeler now, his head bowed, as her voice carried through from somewhere above. *Thy will be done. Thy will be done.*

He heard footsteps on the stairs. His head remained bowed in prayer, reciting psalms. Faith's voice came to him.

"He has to stop with this Methelred."

Anthony thought of bees buzzing.

"He told Miss Marple there's a saint in our walls. Have you ever heard anything so ridiculous?"

"How does he even know what a saint is?"

"Richard, you have to stop his nonsense."

"He's just five, Faith," came the man's voice.

"He's not going to get into the Academy."

"It's not the end of the world if he doesn't."

"It absolutely *is.* Don't you *care* about his future? Good schools.

College, a good job. I want you to call Miss Marple tomorrow."

"I'm not sure getting pushy is…."

"It's not pushy. It's *assertive*. It's being pro-active. And it's the only way to get what you want in life. Be sure to call her tomorrow and let her know how important this is to us. With your raise and bonuses, we can donate to their scholarship fund."

Their voices came into the room full of plants, just outside Anthony's window. The grate was closed.

Thy will be done.

Anthony bowed his head more deeply, thinking of the boy Jacob, and praying for him.

Drifting in the background of his prayers, Faith's voice continued, directing Richard in half a dozen jobs—call Miss Marple, have someone look at the safety of those ruins, get a contractor to look at that stonework in the corner upstairs.

Yes, Anthony thought, *Mr. Long had intended to deal with that corner. Moisture had gotten in. Then he'd caught pneumonia and died soon after.*

She wanted Richard to shop around for therapists for Jacob—and these plants and that awful bedspread in the other room, what should they *do* with them?

Footsteps left the room and her voice drifted away.

Anthony felt his fingertips against his forehead.

Pater noster….

How many times had he said it since being installed here in his cell? It must be hundreds of thousands. He thought of Jacob, who needed him and smiled at his own foolishness in seeking his own will.

Yes, God's will be done, for God knew what *Jacob* needed.

Chapter 6

You have scalded the dragon's head with boiling water, that is with hot tears.

– Ancrene Wisse

Jacob pulled on his pajamas and crawled into bed. It had been days— maybe even a week—Jacob really wasn't good at this time thing—and Mama was still mad at him. She told him to tell the truth. But she got mad when he did. He didn't understand why she hated Methred so much. Methred was a good king.

The window was open beside him. Julio's mother had told him Minnesota was very, very cold. But it was warm. It was even hot and sticky today. Mama told him to open the window for air. A breeze floated in—and also voices.

Jacob climbed to his knees and pressed his face to the window. He found he was looking straight into the window of the house next door. *Next store. Neck store. Neck's door?* The words went through his mind. Why were houses called *next store*? His eyes adjusted to the dark outside and the light shining in the window across the fence between the two houses.

A group of children piled together on a bed, with someone Jacob thought must be their mother in the middle of them. There were many boys and the girl with red hair. A boy younger than Jacob held the smallest boy in his arms. The mother read a story about wolves and pigs. Jacob strained to hear her words. The wolf chased the pigs, blowing their houses down until he came up against a pig with a strong house of bricks.

The boys cuddled into their mother.

Jacob wondered where his mother was. She had to talk with Dan, he knew. And she liked what she called *me time* after dinner. She needed to relax.

Jacob leaned closer to the window, straining to hear.

I'll huff and I'll puff...

"And I'll blow your house down!" All the children sang the words together.

The mother continued reading but Jacob could no longer hear the words. He wanted to know what happened to the wolf.

Their father appeared in the doorway, a big man. The children scrambled off the bed, racing to hug him, some of them around the waist, some of them around the knees. Jacob saw the father throw his head back and heard him laugh, before he dropped to his knees and hugged them all in one big circle of his arms.

Then he looked up. His eyes met Jacob's. He smiled and waved. The mother and all the children turned and looked over, too, smiling and waving.

Jacob ducked down under the window sill and wiggled under his covers.

He wondered what it would be like to have an older brother—or a little sister. What would it be like to have a whole bunch of brothers and sisters, all piled together in a bed, laughing?

Maybe then Mama would read stories? He wondered what this wolf was. He didn't know about a wolf blowing houses down. Mama liked him to know things—and maybe Miss Marple would not let him into the Academy Mama liked so much if he didn't know about this wolf chasing pigs?

He thought about his books about space and castles and knights and even animals—but none of his books talked about wolves blowing down houses.

Maybe Anthony, down in the cellar, would tell him. He was disappointed he hadn't had a chance to run to the cellar to talk with Anthony. But he *would!* Then he could impress Miss Marple and Mama would be happy with him.

He stared up at the glow of the dark consolation map Mama had put on his ceiling.

"Ah, Sir Jacob!" Methred strode across the courtyard, clad in his armor. His page ran after him holding his sword and spear, while a stable boy held the reins of two spirited steeds. "I am optimistic that today is the day we defeat the Red Dragon!"

Jacob bowed to his friend and king. "Methred, I believe we need to call our Franciscan father to pray for our mission."

"A fine idea!" Methred said, and turned to call to the crowd. "Send for Father Antoine!" He turned to his horse, stroking its nose, and outlining his plan of attack to Jacob. More knights joined them in the courtyard. Women ringed the area or waved kerchiefs from the castle hallways, two, three, and four stories above, looking down into the courtyard.

Father Antoine arrived and the knights knelt, holding their hands together on the hilts of their swords.

Knights knelt. Nights knelt. Nights knelled, Jacob thought.

A bell tolled. He bowed his head as Father Antoine intoned a blessing over the army, laying hands on each head.

Jacob raised his head when Father Antoine stopped at him. Their eyes met, Father Antoine's a deep brown. "You must know the Wolf," Father Antoine told him.

"The Wolf?" Jacob asked. Beside him, his horse nudged his shoulder.

"Aye, the Wolf. Only through the Wolf will you know and defeat the Red Dragon."

"But the Dragon is the bigger threat."

"Ah, Sir Jacob, you are wise for your years. But you must still learn that it starts with the small things. And the small things become bigger things. Watch the *Wolf*."

Jacob bowed his head. "Thank you, Father."

He had no idea what the priest was talking about.

Methred's army rode out in splendid array, with banners flying and fine steeds tossing their heads. Each horse wore Methred's glorious blue and white colors, matching the knights' tunics. Jacob and Methred, brothers in all but fact, rode at their head, behind the standard bearer. Jacob sat tall, his ears and eyes filled with the shouts of the girls of the castle, and their waving kerchiefs.

"You are quiet today, brother Jacob," Methred said.

"It is a momentous day," Jacob replied. "Never before have we been so sure of the Red Dragon's whereabouts. We have a large number of men to fight him. Perhaps today *is* the day."

"Let us pray it is. We've the blessing of Father Antoine."

Suddenly, as they approached the village of Malborg, villagers came running out, screaming. "Allaidh! Madah-allaidh!" they shouted.

Methred tensed. "The Wolf!"

"You know of this wolf?" Jacob asked.

"It was only a rumor," Methred said. "I wasn't sure."

"Father Antoine spoke of...."

A woman dropped to her knees, shouting, "The boy, the boy!" and pointing back to the town.

Jacob and Methred, as one, spurred their horses, driving them into the village, swords drawn, ready to fight. As their destriers thundered into the main street, they saw a child, no more than six, cowering back against a wall, as a large wolf, nearly as big as their own steeds, inched nearer, snarling at the terrified boy.

Jacob spurred his horse harder, driving in as the wolf drew a deep breath, huffing. He leaned low, scooping up the frightened child as his horse charged. He knew Methred was right behind, slashing, driving the vicious beast away. He gripped the boy tightly, yanking on his reins, and the great steed wheeled and turned, snorting, and charged again out of the village, as Methred leaned over his horse's neck, snarling back at the animal and raising his sword against it.

Jacob raced on his horse, clinging to the boy, till his animal skidded to, before the frightened villagers. "Whose child is this?"

The woman who had called out about *the boy* came forward. "He's an orphan, Sir."

Jacob looked around the townspeople.

The same woman fell to her knees. "Sire, Sir, I will take him in!" The boy ran into her arms, which wrapped around him, and a cluster of children enveloped the boy and the woman, clinging to both. The woman looked up to Jacob and smiled. "He will have many brothers and sisters to love him now," she said.

At that moment, Methred rode out from the village, looking grim. "The Wolf escaped," he gasped. "Build up your walls to guard against him until we can help you. We must first conquer the Red Dragon."

The people cheered.

Jacob stared at the orphan boy, now surrounded by a family. His heart swelled. He would conquer the Red Dragon and make life good for these people.

He and Methred rode forth, their army behind them.

"Eggs, Jacob?" Daddy stood up from the table, picking up his egg-stained plate.

Mama turned from the stove as Jacob wandered into the kitchen. The stone walls there reminded him of Methred's castle. Mama's garnet bracelet glinted on her wrist.

Jacob climbed up on a chair at the table. A plate waited for him there.

"First Fourth of July in the Twin Cities," Daddy said. "What do you think about going to see the fireworks, Faith?"

Mama shook her head. "I have to be up early tomorrow."

"Maybe I could just take Jacob, then."

Mama shook her head again. "I don't want him getting off his sleep schedule."

"It's just one night. He'll be fine by the time school starts."

Mama shook her head sharply. Daddy shrugged, ruffled Jacob's hair, and left the kitchen.

"Mama, why do wolves hate pigs?"

"Hm?" She turned from the stove, sliding eggs from a pan onto the plate in front of him. "I don't think wolves think about pigs very much."

"Oh."

"Toast?" she asked. At the same moment she poured orange juice into the glass by his plate.

"But don't wolves eat pigs?"

"Wolves are in the forests quite a bit north of here and pigs are on farms. They're never anywhere near each other."

"But don't wolves huff and...."

Mama's phone beeped. "One minute, Jacob." She picked up her phone. "Hey, Dan...no, I'm not busy." She turned, as she listened to Dan on speaker phone, to get the toast as it popped up from the toaster and slathered butter on it. She dropped it in front of Jacob and disappeared into the big dining room.

He could hear her voice as she talked. She was annoyed with Dan. He wasn't very good at his job, Jacob thought. There was that page at Dun Aoibhneas who kept messing up. Methred had moved him to the bakery and then he did very well.

"Some people just aren't born for some jobs," Father Antoine had said, as he savored the page-turned-baker's bread, which was better than any in the castle. "Put people where they're born to be and let their gifts shine, instead of finding fault."

Mama should put Dan on a job he was good at. Maybe he was better at baking than making companies look good. That's what Mama did, she said. She made companies look good so people would want to do business with them. "Like buy things from them," she explained. "I tell them what to say and do so people like them." It was called *pee-are*.

"Methred says people like other people who are good and kind and do the right thing," Jacob said.

Mama tilted her head and quirked one corner of her mouth into a smile. "Methbred isn't real but, yes, that's good I guess, but companies need to know what it is people want and then do it so people will like them."

Jacob thought of Methred and Father Antoine. People liked them because they were good and kind. Jacob tried to be good and kind at Dun Aoibhneas and people seemed to like him, too. He didn't have to ask them what they wanted.

He used his knife to cut his toast into the rough shape of a horse and galloped it around the egg. This way, that way—they would circle the Red Dragon, perhaps. He climbed his toast-horse high up above his plate and suddenly he had an idea. There was a cliff there, above the dragon's lair. Maybe they could post troops up there, and attack it as it emerged. Roll rocks down on its head.

The wolf huffed and puffed. He thought about that—but didn't see how that could help them. You couldn't blow down a cave. Huff and puff and roll rocks down in front of the den to block the dragon in?

Mama was still talking to Dan in the other room. Jacob dove his toast horse into the egg yolk. "We have to swim across the river," he said, "to reach the Red Dragon's lair from a new direction. Maybe he won't see us coming this way." Pepper was a strong horse and a good swimmer, and Sir Jacob was not afraid of the water. His plan would work well. Methred would be pleased with it.

"Jacob!"

Jacob's head shot up.

Mama stashed her phone in the pocket of her red suit coat. "Stop playing with your food. Look what a mess you've made of your fingers!"

"It's a horse," Jacob said.

Mama marched to the sink, where she wet a towel, and came back to scrub the yolk off his fingers. "Manners, Jacob, *manners!* What will I *do* with you? Now, we have interviews set up with three possible nannies this afternoon. I'll be in my office working. I want you cleaned and in your dress shirt, *with a tie,* by two-forty-five. I want you to make a good impression."

"Does that mean I need to do and say the right thing so the nanny will want to do business with us?" Jacob looked up at his mother.

She smiled and touched his cheek. "Yes, Jacob. We want to make a good impression." She glanced at his freshly cleaned fingers. "Nannies want boys who are well-behaved. Not playing with their food." Her face grew stern. "And let's not say there are people in our walls, okay? We don't want to scare the nannies off."

Jacob nodded.

Mama deftly cleared his plate, scraping the last of the egg into the garbage, rinsing the plate, and sticking it in the dishwasher. She left and Jacob jumped off his chair, spreading his arms and flying like the Red Dragon, into the huge middle hall between the front door and the matching doors at the back of the house that went out to the back porch. He could hear Mama in her office. The keys on her computer keyboard *tap-tap-tapped*. A man's voice sounded. She was *zooming*. The Red Dragon *zoomed*. He was always just a little bit too fast for Jacob and Methred and their men. But Jacob's plan would change that!

He zoomed down the stairs to the basement—being quiet as he passed Mama's office at the top of the stairs—and into the Garden Room. "Are you there, Anthony?" he asked.

The window slid open and Anthony was smiling behind the bars. "I'm always here."

Jacob wrapped his fingers around the bars. "Mama thinks Methred isn't real."

"Doesn't she?" Anthony asked.

Jacob shook his head. "Father Antoine says to put people where they work best but she won't do that with Dan and if she knew Methred and Father Antoine are real, maybe she'd find what Dan is good at. But she doesn't believe they're real. Why not?"

"People believe what they want to believe," Anthony said. "They have a view of how they think the world is and sometimes they're not quite ready yet to see that it's a little bit different than they thought."

"Oh." Jacob thought about that. He could feel the Red Dragon beside him, restless. "But Methred *is* real."

"Indeed he is," Anthony said. "And people still believe only when they're ready to. It seems you have a very restless dragon on your hands. Perhaps he needs to fly."

"He does," Jacob said.

Jacob spread his wings and zoomed up the stairs, running down the hall past the huge bookcase full of Daddy's law books and what Mama called *the Great Classics,* and into Daddy's office with the round windows, and out again, and down more halls, hissing and breathing fire.

He lit in the first-floor screened in porch, the one just under his bedroom. The windows were thrown open, letting a nice breeze through the screens. This porch had the outdoor wicker couch from their patio in California, and an oval glass-topped table. Jacob clambered to his knees on the couch. From here, he could see into the yard next door.

The children jumped on the trampoline. The girl bounced up and down, laughing, her braids flying up and down with her. Two of the boys bounced with her, now and again tumbling to their knees and laughing.

Three more boys ran around the yard with swords glinting in the sun. No—four. No, three? Jacob counted again. A boy dashed out from under the trampoline. Five? Suddenly, the oldest of them pointed at him. All the children stopped what they were doing, looking at his window. They all waved.

Jacob's heart almost stopped. He didn't know how to make friends. Methred would wave and smile. Jacob gave a quick wave and scrambled down off the wicker couch. He spread his wings and zoomed away, up to the third floor. Here, there were two more bedrooms in striped wallpaper and the *ballroom* Mama was so proud of and another kitchen and windows looking down to the backyard far below.

Jacob zoomed around the big ballroom. Maybe his soccer ball would finally show up in one of the last boxes soon and he could bring it up here. He saw a lone chair and pushed it to the windows. Standing up tall, he could see the round fountain in his own yard and the children far below, once more bouncing on the trampoline and chasing each other with swords. He wondered what their names were.

A woman came out on the back porch, calling something. Her laugh carried up to the third floor, where the windows were open. It was the same woman who had read about the wolf and the pigs. She glanced up at the sky and Jacob could see she was smiling. The children bounced off the trampoline to the grass and ran up the porch, waving their silver swords.

The alarm went off on Jacob's watch. He dutifully turned it off and ran back down the stairs to his closet for his shirt and tie.

Chapter 7

Do you know what dazes the feeble eyes of people who have climbed up high? That they look downward. Just in the same way, whoever looks at those who are inferior in life comes to think they are superior in life. But always look upward, toward heavenly people who climbed so high— and then you will see how low you stand.

– Ancrene Wisse

Friends. In his cell, on his knees, Anthony bowed his head in prayer. Prayer for the deceased. Prayer for the remaining Long family. Prayer for the Shorter family now living in the house. His thoughts and prayer became stuck on Faith. He pressed himself to pray for her. He chastised himself, knowing his heart was anything but pure. He disliked her in his space. He could feel her presence, like a toxic vapor.

Friends. The word came to him again.

Bring friends for Jacob, he prayed. Another *Ave. Teach him how to make friends,* he prayed. *Give him confidence and courage.*

"Did you like Mrs. Channing?" Mama asked at dinner.

Jacob shook his head. Mrs. Channing had gray hair and a big mole on her chin and told him during the interview to sit up straight. She had asked what he liked to eat and told Mama she would see that he had healthy food as his snack after school.

"I like Miss Grace," Jacob said.

Mama shook her head. "She won't teach you proper manners."

"But you asked me who I *like*. I like *her*. She smiled."

"Smiling's important," Daddy said. "He's going to be spending a lot of time with her so…."

"You'll like Mrs. Channing," Mama said to Jacob. "You'll see she's really very good." To Daddy she said, "She has an excellent resume. She's worked with the best families in St. Paul, including two state senators and the CEO of Pillsbury. She can start in two weeks. We'll just have to make do until then. Jacob, use your knife to cut your salmon."

They ate silently for several minutes at the long table in the big dining room, Jacob swinging his feet under his chair before saying, "Mama, there are a bunch of kids next door."

Mama sniffed and shook her head. "I've noticed. My gosh, that poor woman!"

"What poor woman?"

"Their mother, of course."

"Is their father also poor?"

Daddy laughed as he spooned thinly sliced carrots onto Jacob's plate. "That's not what your mother means. She means she feels sorry for their mother."

Jacob tilted his head, watching his mother as she lifted a bite of lemon and garlic salmon to her mouth. "Why do you feel sorry for her?"

"Well, because she has so many kids!" Mama gave a little laugh as if that should be obvious.

Jacob didn't understand. "We have a big house. It would be fun to have a brother or a sister."

Mama rolled her eyes with a smile. "One is enough for me!" She took a sip of her white wine. "Children are expensive. And I need to be able to work."

"So we can't get a brother or sister?"

Mama laughed. "Good gracious, no, Jacob, we don't just go *get* a brother or sister. That's not how it works."

Jacob frowned. It had worked that way for Julio. He'd gone to his grandmother's for a week and when he came home, they'd gotten a sister, just as they'd told him they would. "How *does* it work?" he asked.

"It works only if a mother and father *want* another child. Jacob, we are quite happy having one child. If we had more, we couldn't give you all the things we want to give you—a nice house, nice clothes, vacations, travel, good schools. A good school is the key to your future. Travel broadens the mind."

Jacob swung his feet under his seat. He thought of the children on the bed and bouncing on the trampoline and their mother laughing on the porch. "I'd rather have a sister. Could we do that if I give up the vacations and house?"

Daddy ruffled his hair. "Sorry, Bud, it's not that easy to just sell a house like this and get a different one. Remember how much work it took to move?"

"Daddy and I need vacations," Mama said. "Our jobs are very stressful." She rubbed her forehead.

"What is *stressful*?"

"When people are demanding a lot of you and it's hard to be happy because you can never relax."

"She looks happy next door," Jacob said. "Maybe you could do her job?"

Mama laughed. "Jacob, she doesn't have a job. She's a *housewife*."

Jacob wasn't sure what that was. Mama made it sound bad, but he almost bounced in his chair, nodding. "But she looks happy! Maybe you could do that, too!"

Mama frowned.

Daddy laughed a little. "Jacob, Mama doesn't *want* to be a stay at home mother."

"Besides, that many kids would only be more stressful!"

Jacob's bouncing stopped. He sighed and pushed a bite of his salmon through the lemon and garlic sauce.

As Jacob lay in his bed that night, a soft knock sounded at his door, and it opened a crack. Daddy stood in the doorway, one finger to his lips, and beckoning with the other hand.

Jacob climbed out of bed. Daddy scooped him up in his arms. "Don't make a sound," he whispered.

Jacob said nothing, as Daddy carried him down the wide front steps to the big room at the bottom. The door to the back yard was ajar. Daddy carefully inched it open and they slipped through onto the back veranda and down the stairs. Two camp chairs waited there, with a little table between them.

The kids ran around the yard next door, shouting in excitement. Daddy waved at the big man with the big mustache who stood on the porch.

"Where's Mama?" Jacob whispered.

"Sleeping," Daddy said. He winked. "Let's keep it that way, okay, Champ?" He set Jacob in one of the chairs and gave him a glass from the table. "Cheers," he said.

They clicked glasses and Jacob drank deeply of the forbidden root beer he loved but was not allowed. At that moment, a grand explosion of lights erupted in the sky, fiery red, white, and blue specks raining down over the city far beyond their back yard.

Jacob gasped in delight.

From the porch and trampoline and yard next door came the *oohs* and *aahs* of all those kids.

"Happy Fourth of July, Jacob," Daddy said.

Jacob woke early the next day. As Mama handed him toast, Daddy winked at him. He smiled, holding tight the secret of the night's fireworks.

"Those kids," Mama said. "They kept me up with their shouting about the fireworks."

"It's just one night, Faith," Daddy said.

Mama pressed two fingers to her temple and drew in a sharp breath. "I have work. It's one night I could have used some rest. Jacob, you'll be going to a summer art camp this week. Eat quickly and get ready and I'll drive you over."

"What is art camp?" Jacob asked.

"Where you learn to appreciate art."

"I don't...."

"Daddy and I really need more time to work. You need to do something until Mrs. Channing can start. Now don't dawdle." She *clip-clipped* out of the room, grabbing for her long red cardigan as she did.

Several nights later, after a day of looking at paintings of ballerinas and ships floating above other ships reflected upside down in the water, and women looking in mirrors at themselves, and making his own painting of a reflection, Jacob took his bath. As soon as he got in the water, he wondered if there was a mirror image of his own bathtub with a boy just like himself turned upside down underneath his tub.

The more he thought about it, the more it made sense. After all, all those ships had ships upside down underneath them in the water and he had a pirate ship floating in the tub. He opened the drain and stuck his face in the water, calling, "Hello?"

The words bubbled back up at him as the water began to circle. Nobody answered.

"Hello!" he called again. He tried several more times, with no success. The water began swirling and making its sucking noise as it went down. He stuck his ear to the drain, thinking maybe a boy on the other side was calling back and he just couldn't hear.

Then he thought maybe it was for the best. Maybe the pirates in the upside down ship weren't as friendly as his. He slapped the drain closed to keep them in and jumped out of the tub.

Mama appeared in the doorway as he wrapped the towel around his waist. "That was awfully quick," she said. "Did you actually take a bath?"

Jacob nodded solemnly. "See my pirate ship?"

"Why is the drain closed?" Mama asked. She leaned over to let the last of the water out. Jacob held his breath, hoping the bad pirates wouldn't come up through the drain.

"Sleep well, Jacob," Mama said. She gave him a quick kiss on the top of his head and left the room. As soon as he heard her talking to Daddy, he slapped the drain closed. Then again, there might be giant squid on the other side. Maybe he should leave it open so the other boy and the pirate ship could escape.

He inched it open—but he ran quickly to his bedroom in case the pirates *were* bad.

In his room, Jacob knelt on his bed and quietly lifted his window as he did every night, hearing one fantastical story after another, unlike anything in his books. He was careful to stay back from the window, where they wouldn't see him. Their mother sat on the bed with a pile of the children around her and two on her lap reading from a new book. Her voice drifted easily across the narrow space between the two open windows. Jacob was curious. He'd never heard of eggs or ham being green. He leaned closer, squinting to try to see the pictures.

Finally, he grabbed his binoculars out of his cubby and leaning close to the window, he could sort of make it out. It seemed to be a strange little creature wearing a hat, chasing another holding a plate.

Then suddenly all the kids started reciting together, loudly, "I do not like them in a house, I do not like them with a mouse! I do not like them here or there, I do not like them anywhere!"

One of the older boys stood up and delivered the last lines on his own, with a fist to his chest. "I do not like green eggs and ham!" He stuck a finger in the air, and aimed his nose at the ceiling, proclaiming grandly, "I *do not like them*, Sam I Am!"

All the kids laughed.

They did it over and over, Jacob inching closer to the window, opening the screen, and leaning out a little to try to see the pictures through his binoculars. He was sad when the story ended. And surprised to find that green eggs and ham were quite tasty.

The mother kissed and hugged the kids, tucked them into several beds, including a bunk bed. She wiggled her hand in front of her face and they all murmured together. Then she looked out the window, smiled and waved, and called out, "Sleep well!"

Jacob yanked his head back in and scrambled under his covers. He thought about Mama's comments about *stressful*. Sometimes he and Methred liked to sneak away from the castle to the river that flowed behind it, down at the bottom of a steep hill, and fish and bring their catch for the castle cooks. Kings didn't typically fish—but he and Methred enjoyed it after weeks of fighting the Red Dragon and dealing with all the other business of the kingdom.

He guessed he saw what Mama meant by *stressful*.

But it seemed that happy, laughing kids and bouncing on a trampoline and reading books at night would be a nice break from *stressful*, just like fishing was.

But Mama didn't think so. Jacob decided he'd talk to Anthony about it.

Chapter 8

So tears with heartfelt prayers are good—and if you follow, I have here described four great effects for which they ought to be loved. In all your needs send these messengers at once quickly toward heaven. For as Solomon says, The prayer of the humble pierces the heavens and St. Augstine adds, O great is the power of a shining and pure prayer, which flies up and comes in before Almighty God and does her errand so well that God has all she says written in the books of life.

– Ancrene Wisse

It was a few more days before Jacob could get down to see Anthony again. Mama whisked him off to his art camp early every morning. He spent all day in a big museum learning about art and doing his own drawings and paintings, learning French from Miss DuBois, and one day listened to an *ork-straw*—a bunch of people playing music together. They played a story about a boy named Peter Andrew Wolf.

He came home to dinner and took his bath, always trying to talk to the boy on the other side, and went to bed—where he listened to stories next door, being more careful to stay back against the wall where they wouldn't see him—only to be up early the next day.

He sometimes thought he heard *God's will be done* at night.

On Friday after art camp, in the downstairs sun room below his bedroom, he managed to get a look into the house next door at dinner time. The parents sat at either end of a very long table, with five children on either side. They all suddenly waved their hands around their faces, then bowed their heads over clasped hands. A few moments later, all of them waved their hands around their faces and shoulders again. It reminded Jacob of the musicians. Somehow, they all knew to pick up their instruments at the same time and all the violin bows knew how to move together. It fascinated him.

Suddenly, a big girl, much older than Jacob, looked up, saw him, and waved with a big smile. All the others turned.

Jacob scrambled off the chair, and ducked down to the floor to crawl away, where they couldn't see him watching them.

"Jacob! What are you doing?"

Jacob lifted his eyes from Mama's black heels past her straight red skirt to her black blazer. She frowned down at him. "Get up. You're getting dust on your clothes! Why are you on the floor?"

"They looked at me," Jacob said.

"Who did? Not more of your imaginary friends?" She slipped off one, then the other, of her heels, and sighed in relief.

"No, the kids next door."

Mama glanced out the window. "They're eating dinner. How were they looking at you?"

Jacob felt his face redden. "I was looking at them," he admitted. "They all waved their hands over their faces—twice—before they ate. What was that, Mama?"

"Come on to the table," Mama said. She took his hand and they walked side by side into the kitchen, where Daddy had shrimp on the stove and plates on the table.

"Hey, my favorite people are here!" Daddy looked happy to see them. He kissed Mama on the cheek and just for a moment, she smiled. "How was work?" Daddy asked.

Mama sighed again. "Dan doesn't seem happy with anything and my boss is breathing down my neck."

"How was camp, Champ?" Daddy ruffled his hair. "Are you learning poetry?"

"What's poetry?"

"Rhyming words. Like Camp Champ." Daddy laughed.

Mama rolled her green eyes. "There's far more to poetry than that. That's not even a limerick. We could perhaps discuss Yeats and Keats."

"Yeets and Keets," Daddy said. "They rhyme, too." He winked at Jacob.

Mama sighed. "You *know* it's not pronounced like that."

Daddy sprinkled a bit of something over the shrimp and stirred it. "Yates and Kates."

"Did you do some art today?" Mama ignored Daddy.

Jacob nodded.

"Well, go get it."

Jacob hesitated.

"Go on." Mama lifted a bottle and poured herself a glass of white wine.

Jacob ran off to get the picture he had drawn. "Today was colored pencils." He climbed up on his chair and put the picture out in front of Mama.

She stared at the castle with the big dragon flying over it and the two horsemen below. She cleared her throat.

"Nice castle," Daddy said, looking over her shoulder.

"I hope you didn't tell them that's...."

"Garlic, lemon, and chives!" Daddy said. He brought the pan to the table. He tilted it, sliding shrimp and linguine onto Jacob's plate, and then Mama's.

Mama picked up her fork. No waving hands.

"Why did they wave their hands like that?" Jacob asked.

"What?" Daddy dished up his own linguine and sat down.

"Who?" Mama asked.

"The people next door."

"With that many kids, they're probably Catholic," Mama said.

"What's Catholic?"

"Like the Cathedral down the street."

"The kids jumped on the trampoline all the time. They don't seem weak," Jacob said.

"Huh?" Daddy removed his glasses, staring at Jacob.

"So they were probably praying." Mama took a deep drink of her white wine.

"What's praying?"

Mama stabbed delicately at a shrimp with her fork. Her red nails caught the kitchen light. "Talking to an invisible friend in the sky and believing it's real."

Jacob swirled thin pasta around his fork. Mama always said he had invisible friends but he knew they were real. So he guessed he was praying...maybe? But then what was the difference between praying and talking?

"Now let's not be quite so cynical." Daddy said.

"Religion is for people too weak to face life on their own," Mama replied.

"What is religion?" Jacob asked.

"Believing in gods—powerful beings that don't exist. Greek mythology, for instance, says Zeus is the god of the skies. His brother Poseidon is god of the seas. He either helps sailors or hurts them, depending if they've been good to him or not. Now we clearly know there's no old man with a pitchfork in the sea, right, Jacob?"

Jacob nodded. But he thought it would be fun to play Poseidon in his bathtub with his toy boats. Maybe one of his knights could wear a crown and be Poseidon. He wondered if the boy on the other side of the tub had a knight to play Poseidon. Maybe there was a real Poseidon on the other side of the tub. He contemplated as he took a mouthful of linguine. "Are gods powerful like a dragon?" he asked. "Dragons are powerful."

"No. Gods are different than dragons. They're all-knowing. They can help people or hurt people."

"So can a dragon."

"But a god is stronger than a dragon. Gods can do things like control wind and rivers or throw lightning bolts."

Jacob pushed his linguine across his plate. "So if you wanted to fight a dragon, you would need a god?"

Mama pushed a hand through her hair and took a quick sip of her white wine. "Well, if either of them existed and you were fighting a dragon, I suppose so. But neither gods nor dragons exist." She leaned forward suddenly, grasping Jacob's hand. "Jacob, in this world, we have only ourselves to depend on. That's *why* it's so important to give you the best education, the best schools, to have you meet the right people—so you have a good life ahead of you!"

Daddy laid a hand on Jacob's arm. "Jacob, Mama is tired. Let's not talk about dragons and gods, okay, Bud?"

"Sure, Daddy." Jacob swung his legs under his stool and stabbed three small shrimp on his fork, gulping them in one bite.

"Small bites, Jacob. Manners."

"Yes, Mama." He wondered what story the kids would read tonight. Maybe he should talk to Methred about finding a god to help them fight this Red Dragon.

He brought it up in their tent that night as they lay in their cots. "Methred, what do you know of the Greek gods, of Zeus and Poseidon?"

Methred turned, staring at Jacob in the light of the candle that burned between their two cots. "We certainly learned of them growing up."

"Gods are powerful. Why have we not sought the help of one in fighting the Red Dragon?"

Methred laughed. "We know well, in our day, that the Greek gods of mythology were not real. I'm surprised you would ask such a thing, Jacob."

Jacob wanted to ask, *So there are no gods?* But he felt this was something he should know in Methred's world. Sometimes, not often, but every once in awhile, it seemed, he was just a child in another, far-away land, and didn't know the things a knight should know.

Methred saved him the difficulty of answering. "When Paul was in Athens, he saw altars and temples to many gods. Among those was one strange altar that caught his attention. On it were inscribed the words *To the Unknown God*. Paul told the Greeks that this Unknown God of theirs was the One True God. God the Father of Jesu Christi. It is His protection we seek. That is *who* Father Antoine has been asking for help."

"Why hasn't He helped us these two years?" Jacob asked.

Methred chuckled. "He will, Jacob." He blew out the candle, sinking the tent into darkness. "He will."

Jacob woke to sunlight pouring in his window. Saturday! No summer camp! He bolted out of bed and jumped astride Pepper, who waited patiently by his bed. They galloped out his bedroom door with Barkee racing along beside them, woofing happily, and past the long stretch of book shelves full of Mama and Daddy's books on so many Important Things, toward the big main stairs.

"Jacob," Daddy called from his office at the top of the stairs, "I'm working. I have some zoom meetings in a couple minutes here. Try to keep it down."

"Okay, Daddy!" Jacob and Pepper skidded to a halt, Pepper blowing his nose hard with the exertion and thrill. "Can we go out and see the ruins today?"

Daddy turned from his computer. He looked tired. "Hey, Bud, I'm sorry. I'm not sure today is going to work out. I still have lots of meetings to get up and running after the time I took off for the move. Why haven't you gone out there yourself?"

Jacob shrugged. From the porch, the yard looked like it fell right down into the city and the Sippy river. He didn't want to admit to Daddy that he wasn't sure what to do about that. "I'd rather go with you," he said.

"Maybe we could try for tomorrow." He looked so sad.

"It's okay, Daddy," Jacob said. "Pepper and I will go find it." Pepper and Barkee knew this land. With them, he'd probably be safe. "I'll tell you about it."

Daddy smiled. "Who's Pepper?"

"My horse." Jacob patted the brilliant ebony mane of his beautiful steed. "He's a very fine horse!"

Daddy's smile grew. "I bet he is! How are you liking that 'cellar?' You could ride your scooter or a bike down there in the winter. We can move that bed out to give you space."

"I'm going down now to talk with Anthony," Jacob said.

Daddy laughed. "Well, have a good talk. Tell him hi from me."

"I will," Jacob promised.

Daddy's smile fell. "Hey, Bud?"

Jacob waited.

"Can you tell me about Pepper and Anthony—and maybe not tell Mama about them?"

Jacob's smile fell. "She thinks I'm making them up."

"It's only that she's stressed at work," Daddy said. "She just doesn't understand some things because she's thinking about problems at work."

Jacob thought for a fleeting moment that maybe Mama would be happier if she talked to Anthony. But he shrugged. "Okay, Daddy." He wheeled his great steed and they tip-toed quietly down the big stairs and across the hall to the smaller stairs.

In the cellar, Jacob dismounted outside the Garden Room. It had once been where the laundresses did their work, Anthony had told him. Those peculiar machines that pulled in and out of the wall—they had dried the big, heavy clothes of the late 19th Century.

Jacob had barely stepped into the room before the panel in the wall slid back, revealing bars and Anthony's face behind them, smiling.

"Anthony!" Jacob ran up to the bars, grasping them between his hands. "I had to go to summer camp all week. Then I had to have dinner and a bath and go to bed. Were you lonely?"

Anthony smiled more broadly. "I am never lonely. Well, rarely. I am in the presence of God day and night and always praying."

Jacob glanced around the room and spotted a wooden stool. He pulled it to the window and climbed up so he could sit face to face with Anthony.

"What is praying? Mama says it's talking to an invisible friend in the sky."

Anthony chuckled. "Well, I suppose she's right. Praying *is* talking. And God is not visible to most of us, most of the time. And we do say His home is in the Heavens which I suppose is, in some sense, in the sky."

"What is visible?"

"Things you can see with your human eyes. Some things, like air, we can't see with our eyes, but we know they exist."

"Mama can't see Methred," Jacob said.

"And yet he's real, isn't he?" Anthony asked. "As is the air you breathe. What we see with our eyes is not all there is of this world."

Jacob nodded vigorously. "Why do you talk to God?" he asked. "Is He the Greeks' Unknown God?"

"Paul certainly believed he was," Anthony said. "I tend to think so, too. And why do I talk to Him? Why do you talk to your parents?"

"Because I love them," Jacob said. "Because they love me and they tell me things I need to know."

Anthony smiled. "Like what?"

"Like how important school is to my future."

Anthony smiled softly. "Yes, school teaches us what we need to know for this life. And that's why I talk to God. He loves me and tells me things I need to know for the next life."

"Like what?"

"Like how important it is to love Him, to love other people, to try to put good into the world."

"What is the next life?" Jacob asked.

"The next life is really just the rest of this life," Anthony said. "What we on earth call dying is only moving on."

"Daddy says some people don't know they've died," Jacob said. "So they stay around as ghosts. Do you think that's true?"

"There are many things we don't understand," Anthony said.

Jacob tilted his head. "But if we know we died, where do we go?"

"To God's wonderful mansions in the Heavens."

"I live in a mansion!" Jacob said excitedly.

Anthony's smile grew. "Ah, yes, you do. But if you can believe it, the mansions in Heaven are a thousand times more beautiful!"

Jacob's eyes grew round. "Do they have ruins, too? Daddy says we have ruins in the back yard. And there's a fountain there."

"There may be fountains in heaven," Anthony said. "I haven't been there—because I haven't died. But there are no ruins because nothing ever decays or dies there."

Jacob thought of the men who had died fighting the Red Dragon. "Are there Dragons there?" he asked. "What happens if we need to fight dragons there?"

"If there are dragons, they're full of love, and good to people," Anthony replied.

"Is that what happened to my men who died fighting the Red Dragon? Did they go to the next world?"

"I would think so." Anthony leaned close to the grate. The sunlight reflected in his eyes. "I think they are happy in Heaven with God. They are martyrs after all. They gave their lives for the sake of others."

"Should I be talking to God to help me with the Red Dragon?"

Anthony smiled and reached his fingers through the grate.

Jacob wove his fingers into the monk's.

"Yes," Anthony said. "Talk to God and He will help you with all that you need because He loves you."

"I need a friend here," Jacob said. "I didn't make any friends at summer camp. They all knew each other already."

"Go next door," Anthony suggested. "You'll find friends there."

"Do you know them?" Jacob asked.

Anthony grinned. "Indeed I do. They are the Lovard family. They are loving and welcoming and you don't need to be afraid of them. Just treat them like you would treat Methred."

"I told Mama it would be fun to have a sister. She said *one is enough for her!*"

"Then let's pray for that sister, shall we?" Anthony waved his hand over his face like the Lovards had done, then pressed his hands together, palm to palm. "Dear Lord Jesus," he said softly, "A little girl would bring so much happiness to this family. If that's Your will, we pray for Jacob to have a little sister." He opened his eyes, smiling.

"Is that all?" Jacob asked.

"That's all," Anthony said. "And you can pray, too. In fact, you should." He looked over at the plants. "And just like planting a seed— sometimes it takes a little bit and it seems like it will never happen—and then suddenly you see the answer to your prayer!"

"Thank you, Anthony!" Jacob's smile grew. "I'm going out to see the fountain. Do you want me to bring you anything?"

"A piece of cheese would be nice," Anthony said.

Their hands slipped apart.

Chapter 9

When a castle or town is assailed, those within pour scalding water out, and so guard the walls. And you should do just the same as often as the enemy assails your castle and the city of the soul: with heartfelt prayers, pour out scalding tears over him ...

– Ancrene Wisse

Jacob mounted Pepper and they galloped up the stairs, being quiet at the top so as not to disturb Mama in her office. He could see her hunched over her computer with two fingers pressed against her temple. She let out a heavy sigh.

Jacob and Pepper crept around the corner, then galloped through the huge square Hall Between the Rooms, out through the gigantic back doors onto the red-stone veranda.

They trotted down the steps that led to the back yard which was so different from his back yard in California. Metal stairs led to a big circular flagstone patio, surrounded by low hedges, with a fountain in the middle. Inside the fountain a red stone horse half reared and water shot up from somewhere, raining back down over the horse.

Jacob ran down the stairs. He would be brave and go with Pepper to where the yard fell off into the city, and find the ruins. But first, he leaned over the stone wall, swirling his hand through the water around the horse, telling himself he would be brave. Goldfish swam in the water. They chased after his hand as he trailed it through the crystal water.

The sound of laughter distracted him. He looked up. Over the chain link fence, the kids next door jumped on the trampoline. He could hardly count them as they bounced like popcorn popping. There was the girl with the red hair—and a couple of boys. And two more boys ran around the yard, ducking behind the big tree, shooting at each other with Nerf guns.

"Pow, pow!" shouted one boy.

"Bang! Bang-bang-bang, *ka-zhoo!*" the other yelled back.

Jacob smiled. Anthony's words reassured him.

The girl did a big flip in the air and bounced right off the trampoline. Faster than the Red Dragon, she was at the fence, waving at Jacob. "Come over and play with us!"

The boys with the Nerf guns stopped their battle and raced, too, to the fence, climbing halfway up and leaning over. "Can we see your goldfish?"

"Do you throw pennies in it for wishes?"

"Mom said we can't come over unless you invite us. Could you invite us?"

"Is there really a ballroom on your top floor!"

Jacob glanced over his shoulder. Mama was in her office. Daddy was busy with work. They wouldn't want to be interrupted.

"I don't know," he said.

"You don't know if you throw pennies in?" One of the boys dug in his pocket, finding a penny. "Bet I can make it in from here!"

Jacob found himself smiling, despite feeling overwhelmed by all of them. So he said what he said when Methred boasted he could beat him in a race or at jousting. "Bet you can't!"

"It's on!" The boy narrowed his eyes, while his sister and brothers began clapping and cheering him on. He held the penny like he was about to skip a stone, drew a deep breath and snapped his wrist. The penny shot to the middle of the pond, disappearing under the fountain's spray, nicked the rearing horse, and splashed into the water.

The kids next door all cheered.

"Your turn!" the boy declared. "You have to come over on this side to make it fair!"

"I don't know if I...." He didn't want Mama to be mad.

"Come on!" the kids all jumped up and down, yelling.

"Just climb over," said the boy who had thrown the penny.

Anthony popped into Jacob's mind and suddenly it seemed like a wonderful idea. He was sure Anthony would approve. Mama was in her office and wouldn't come out for hours. He dug his toes into the chain link and scrambled over, catching his shorts for just a second on the wire on the top.

He took the penny the boy offered and squinted like the boy had done. The kids jumped and cheered for him just as they had for their brother and he felt his chest puff up with pride at their cheers. He flung the penny.

It fell far short of the pond.

"Here, like this," said one of the older boys who had run with a Nerf gun. He showed Jacob how to hold the penny, how to angle his wrist.

The afternoon passed in attempt after attempt, with much laughter, until Jacob finally got two in the fountain. He jumped and laughed as they all patted him on the back or slugged his shoulder.

Then they all ran for the trampoline, scrambling up like monkeys. They bounced together on it, shouting their names.

"Levi!" called the boy who had shown him how to throw pennies.

"Do you know who his favorite composer is?" asked the other older boy.

"What's a composer?" Jacob asked, as the trampoline tossed him back in the air.

"Somebody who writes music!" The girl's braids flew up in the air as she came back down.

"Strauss!" shouted the other older boy. All the kids laughed and started singing some sort of melody at the top of their lungs.

Jacob didn't get it. But he laughed too. They were too happy not to laugh.

"Joseph," shouted the same boy.

"Maria!" shouted the girl.

"Elias!" The boy who had thrown the penny was about Jacob's age.

"Caleb!" The last boy might be Jacob's age or a little younger.

"Jacob," Jacob said.

At that moment, an older girl appeared on the back steps. "The gingerbread is ready!" She smiled at Jacob, saying, "I'm Amanda Lynn."

"Amanda Lynn!" Caleb shouted and rolled off the edge of the trampoline.

"Mandolin! Mandolin!" Levi, Joseph, Maria, and Elias followed, two of them falling to their knees and immediately bouncing up and scrambling up the stairs.

Jacob ran up after them, into a house of dark wood flooring and stone walls inside like his own. The room just inside the back door had library shelves full of books. On the edges of the shelves sat several green dragons made of stone, all of them smiling, unlike the Red Dragon. Jacob stopped, looking at the biggest one, sitting in front of a row of books with colorful spines.

"Is your dad a lawyer, too?" he asked.

"No. He just reads...mostly history," Maria said. "Come on."

In the dining room, the same room Jacob had seen from his house, Amanda Lynn had a bunch of plates of gingerbread with whipped cream set out. She named each plate as she pulled out chairs. "Levi, Joseph, Maria, Jacob, Elias, Caleb."

As Caleb grabbed his fork, Amanda Lynn looked at him sternly. "Wait for prayers." She turned, raising her voice. "Noah, do you want some gingerbread?"

From a hallway, an older boy came racing in, skidding across the floor and seating himself at the table. "Where's Thomas Dylan?"

"Sleeping," said Amanda Lynn. "Mom's with Malachi. Dad's in his office working. Ethan?"

In the corner, a boy even older than Levi looked up from a pile of books. "No thanks. I have to study."

"I'll make an exception this time." Amanda Lynn brought a plate to the boy at the desk and returning, she bowed her head and they all wiggled their hands around their faces and shoulders, speaking in unison.

Jacob stared in amazement. They finished speaking, wiggled their hands again, and dove into their treats, all except for Elias who stared at Jacob and said in shock, "You didn't pray!"

"It's okay, Elias," Amanda Lynn said.

At the same time, Jacob nodded earnestly. "I do too pray! Mama said praying is talking to invisible friends and she says Methred and everyone at Dun Aoibhneas are my invisible friends. Why do you do that with your hands before you talk to your friends?"

Several of the children looked confused. But Amanda Lynn took the seat beside him. "Before we tell God thank you for the food we say *In the name of the Father,*" she touched her head, *"and of the son,"* she touched her chest, *"and of the Holy Spirit."* She touched each shoulder.

"Which father?" Jacob looked around at all the boys. "Which son?" In his family, there was only one father and one son.

Amanda Lynn smiled. "God the Father and Jesus Christ His Son."

"Oh." Jacob took a big bite of gingerbread. He and Methred really needed a god, he thought. Mama had said gods were more powerful than dragons. "You talk to gods?"

"To *the* God." From the desk in the corner, Ethan lifted his head.

"The Unknown God?" Jacob asked.

Amanda Lynn's eyebrows went up. "That's what the Greeks called Him. That's a very impressive thing to know at your age. How old are you?"

"Five," Jacob said. "Almost six! My birthday's in September."

"How do you know about the Greeks calling Him the Unknown God?"

"Methred told me, and Anthony said it's true."

"Who's Anthony?" Elias asked.

"He's the saint in our cellar."

Amanda Lynn tilted her head, her fork paused.

"You have a *saint* in your cellar?" Joseph asked.

"Cool," shouted Levi. "Which one?"

"Anthony."

"St. Anthony who finds lost things?"

"I don't know," Jacob said. "I haven't lost anything."

"Anthony of Padua?"

"I don't know," Jacob said.

"How did he get in your basement?" Maria asked.

"I don't know," Jacob said. "He said Mr. and Mrs. Long wanted him there and he prays for anyone who lives there."

"You talk to him?" Amanda Lynn asked.

Jacob nodded.

"About what?"

"Lots of things. He said school teaches us what we need to know for this life. But we should talk to God because God loves us and teaches us what we need to know for the next life, like to love Him and love other people and put good into the world."

All the kids stared at him.

"He said we should pray."

The Lovard kids nodded eagerly. "We pray all the time!"

"He prayed that I would have a baby sister and said I should pray, too. Will you, too?"

Again, the Lovard kids nodded eagerly.

Amanda Lynn put a hand on Jacob's. "That's amazing, Jacob," she said. "Would you ask Anthony to pray for our family, too?"

Jacob smiled and nodded. He felt warm inside. He was pretty sure he'd made friends!

Chapter 10

Wheat is holy talk, as St. Anselm says. A woman grinds grit when she chatters; her two jaws are the two grinding stones, her tongue is the clapper.

– Ancrene Wisse

Mrs. Channing arrived the next Monday for her first day. The mole on her chin, Jacob was sure, was bigger than ever. She peered at him over glasses with disapproval before assuring Mama he'd be well taken care of and marching him out the door for a long walk, telling him stories of all the grand houses on the street and Important People who had lived in each, and reminding him not to skip or run, but walk like a young gentleman.

While Mama worked, she watched him eat lunch with the sharp eyes of a hawk, correcting his hold on his fork and his posture on his chair and making him wash up the dishes afterward. She sat him at the table in the dining room and opened a book of French in front of him, saying, "I'll expect you to do lessons each evening after I'm gone."

He was relieved when Mama finally emerged from her office, greeting Mrs. Mole with enthusiasm. "We'll certainly be working on posture and several other things," Mrs. Mole informed her. "You will soon have a well-behaved young gentleman on your hands." She headed out the door.

"Come into dinner, Jacob," Mama said.

He followed her into the kitchen, climbing up on the tall stool.

"What is this?" Worn out from his day with Mrs. Channing, Jacob looked at the bowl full of meat and sauce in front of him. Small white orbs floated on top.

"Beef Bourguignon," Mama said. She suddenly spoke like Miss DuBois at the art camp.

Jacob pushed at the white orbs. "Are these mice eyeballs?"

"Jacob!" Mama threw her napkin down in her lap. "Those are *pearl onions!* Beef bourguignon is garnished with *pearl onions.*"

Daddy glanced between them and dug into his bowl. "Mm, good, Faith. Very nice."

"Boogey on," Jacob said. "Why is it called boogey on?"

"Bouh-guh-*non*," Mama said, sounding again like Miss DuBois.

"Booger non?"

Mama sighed. "Richard, maybe we should put him in the French immersion school. This won't do."

"But it looks like stew." Jacob pushed at the *pearl onions.* He wasn't convinced they weren't mice eyeballs.

"Faith, he's *just five.*"

"He's almost six. If not now, when is he supposed to learn these things?"

"But why is it boogoo non and not stew?"

Mama sighed again, a great heave of her breath.

"If you want him to learn, Faith, just tell him. I'm actually curious myself."

"Stew," Mama said, with one eyebrow raised, "is *common.* This is braised in fine Burgundy and garnished with pearl onions, mushrooms, and bacon. It is entirely different."

"Well, it's very good," Daddy said. "What do you think, Jake? You like it?"

Jacob took a bite, avoiding the eyeballs, and nodded. It *was* good. He ate while his parents talked to each other about their jobs. Dan was messing up again.

"Maybe he'd do better as a baker," Jacob said.

Mama's fork paused halfway to her mouth.

Daddy laughed. "Where do you come up with these things, Jacob? He's a marketer, not a baker."

"But maybe he'd be better at baking."

Mama shook her head and rolled her eyes. "I can't really disagree," she said. "He might have a point. Do you know what he did today?"

She and Daddy continued to talk about Dan. Jacob returned to eating carefully around the eyeballs. Mama glanced at the five eyes staring up from the bottom of his bowl and opened her mouth.

"Faith," Daddy said, "The *St. Paul* magazine came today. The cover story is about that author who lives around here, what was his name?"

Mama brightened. "M.M. Love. He's as famous as J.K. Rowling!" She turned to Jacob. "His books are being turned into movies. If we meet him, maybe you could end up with a role! You'd be famous and wealthy!"

Daddy picked a shiny magazine up off the kitchen counter, showing it to her. It had a picture of a man with a big, black mustache in a suit coat, looking very serious. "If you'll put away the food, I'll do the dishes so you can take a glass of wine and go read the magazine. Maybe you'll find out where they live and we can meet them."

"Sounds like I get the better end of the deal." She stood up, and lifted the pot of boogy non. "Jacob, eat your pearl onions."

As she turned, Daddy flashed his spoon out, scooping up the eyeballs, and gulped them down. He winked at Jacob. Jacob smiled back.

Daddy left the kitchen, calling over his shoulder, "Faith, I need to get an email out to that new client. I'll be back in a few to do the dishes."

"Jacob," Mama said, "go take your bath."

"Would you read me a bedtime story after my bath?"

Mama turned from the counter, where she was scraping boogy non and eyeballs into a plastic container. "Jacob, you know I have my me-time after dinner. I've had a long day. I'm going to read that magazine article."

"Yes, Mama." Jacob stared at his empty bowl.

Thy Will Be Done. He looked up at the walls, the ceiling, and down at the floor. Anthony, he thought, was talking to his friend, the Unknown God.

Please give me a little sister, he thought to Anthony's friend.

Mama put the leftovers in the fridge, poured herself white wine, and walked off with the shiny magazine to the living room.

Jacob jumped off his stool and ran up to his room. He brushed his teeth quickly and then, on his knees on his bed, he pushed his window up. The mother was just coming into the bedroom. The children piled on her lap and she opened a book full of bright colors.

Jacob leaned his head against the window frame listening as all the kids chanted together, *Chicka chicka boom boom! Will there be enough room?*

Their mother looked over at him and smiled. Ethan wiggled off the bed and ran to lift their window higher. He waved and Jacob waved back, smiling. He fell asleep to the sound of *chicka chicka boom boom.*

Methred and Jacob gathered with their men at the far edge of the wide plain that spread for a mile or more before the Red Dragon's Cave.

Methred looked around his hundreds of men. "Only yesterday, the Red Dragon took another village child!"

The men roared in anger.

"We have failed our people!" Methred shouted.

"We have tried many times to slay the Red Dragon," one of the men called. "Our friends and brothers have fallen in combat trying to stop him. What more can we do?"

Methred nodded to one of the Franciscan monks.

Jacob's horse moved restlessly beneath him. The monks came in a long line, then dropped to their knees before Methred and Jacob and the waiting army. The abbot lifted his hands over the men, intoning words.

As he stood, Jacob saw the flash of a lower case T hanging from a leather thong around the abbot's neck. It was the same thing Anthony wore around his. Jacob wondered at the coincidence.

And it suddenly dawned on him that he'd never really thought about this ritual they had with the monks before every battle. He didn't have time to think about it now.

Methred was pacing his horse before the men. "Sir Jacob has had a brilliant idea! We have always tried to fight the Red Dragon from the *front* of the cave or while he's already in mid-air. We clearly cannot fight him this way."

He stopped his horse before a group of men from the village that had just lost a child to the monster. "And so this time, we will go up the hill, to the ridge above the cave." He outlined the plan.

The men cheered.

One man stepped forward. "What if the Dragon comes out and sees us marching there? Will he not be forewarned?"

"We have planned for that!" Jacob beamed. "We will pitch our tents here, in his sight. We'll leave a small contingent to make noise and move around so that he believes we're here. The rest will go by night under cover of darkness and start gathering the boulders and rocks to be rolled down at first light."

"Sir Jacob! Sir Jacob!" The cries went up, as the men, for the first time in several years, had hope of actually defeating the monster that menaced their kingdom.

Chapter 11

This is what St. Gregory says: When we join together for the work of prayer it is as though we are holding one another's hands over slippery paths, so that each one may be the stronger for the other's support. Again, in strong winds, or when one must wade through swift waters, each of the company holds onto another.

– Ancrene Wisse

Jacob prayed every day for a baby sister but none showed up. He visited Anthony almost every day after Mrs. Mole left and they talked about hundreds of things as Anthony ate the cheese Jacob brought. About great battles of the past. History. Dragons. The problem of stopping the Red Dragon. The Lovards. The Longs and Anthony's first days in his cell.

Anthony told him stories of great saints and the amazing things they did. Floating in the air! Being in two places at once! "Less dramatic, but more important," Anthony said, "many of them had great powers to heal."

"Do *you* have power to heal?" Jacob asked.

"Well, if someone needs healing, I guess we'll find out!" Anthony smiled. Jacob smiled back. Mrs. Mole was always annoyed with him. But Anthony liked him.

Jacob listened every night to the stories being read next door and they all waved at each other and said good night.

August arrived.

Mama finally had a few days off. "First in forever," she sighed as she came into the kitchen. She looked strange in her jeans and a short-sleeved red shirt, unlike her work clothes. "How about we go to the zoo, Jacob?"

Jacob nodded eagerly, running to climb up on a stool at the tall kitchen table. "Will we take sandwiches?"

"Of course." She smiled as she reached for the coffee maker and filled her mug. "Did you help yourself to some cereal?"

"Daddy made me eggs."

"Very nice."

"Why don't we ever get the green eggs?"

"Hm?" She pulled out her phone. "Eggs aren't green."

"Some are. And they're really good. I would eat them anywhere."

"How would you know? You've never had them because they don't exist." She laughed, then said, "Give me a second here. I need to just double-check work emails." She glanced at the phone a second, then heaved a sigh and left the kitchen. "I'll be right back, Jake."

Jacob sighed. He might not get to the zoo after all. It didn't matter. There were the kids next door to play with. He still hadn't looked for the ruins. He'd continued to be afraid to go by himself, even with Pepper. Maybe they could all go down there.

And of course there was Anthony. Jacob grabbed some cheese out of the refrigerator and ran down to the Cellar. He knocked on Anthony's window. It slid back, revealing Anthony smiling behind the bars.

"I brought you cheese!" Jacob pushed it through the bars.

"Thank you," Anthony said. "What kind is it today?"

"I don't know," Jacob said. "I don't know much about cheese."

"Well, I wouldn't either, except that my father made cheese."

"He did?"

Anthony nodded. "Well, to be precise, the cheese maker on his farm made cheese. Gouda, cheddar, Swiss, all sorts of things."

"What is Gouda?"

"A creamy cow's milk cheese from Holland."

"Doesn't all milk come from cows? My book said milk comes from cows."

Anthony shook his head. "Milk can come from goats, sheep, yaks—lots of animals. Iberico cheese is made from the milk of three of them—goats, sheep, and cows."

"What kind do you like best?" Jacob asked.

"Iberico." Anthony leaned close to the bars. "It was my father's favorite and when I have it, I still think of him."

"I've been playing with the kids next door," Jacob said. "They ask about you all the time. They ask if you're still praying for them."

"I am." Anthony nodded solemnly. "You can, too. Pray particularly for their son Malachi. He's sick."

Jacob nodded eagerly.

"In fact," Anthony added, "God has recently asked me to pray for them, just as I have prayed for you and your parents for the last year."

"But you didn't know us for a year," Jacob said. Then he remembered his parents never came down to the Cellar. "How do you know Mama and Daddy?"

Anthony's eyes raised briefly to the ceiling. "When you spend a lot of time talking to God—and a lot of time *listening* to God—God begins to tell you what He wants you to know."

"Who *is* God?" Jacob asked. "He's not like Poseidon, is he? Mama says there's no man in the ocean with a pitchfork."

"No, there is not," Anthony agreed. "But Poseidon is a story. God is real."

"But who *is* he?" Jacob asked again.

"He is the One Who created this world and us and loves us more than anything."

"Do you see him?"

Anthony took a last bite of cheese. "I have felt His presence in the same way I know you're here. I have seen Jesus. Many times." As Jacob opened his mouth to ask more, Anthony said, "I think your mother might be ready to go to the zoo."

At that moment, Mama's voice came down the stairs. "Jacob? Are you down there?"

"Say hello to the pachyderms for me!"

"What are packy-derms?"

"Elephants." Anthony slid the window shut, hiding any sign of the bars.

Jacob jumped on Pepper and galloped up the stairs, nearly colliding with Mama at the top, in her jeans and bright red shirt.

"Jacob! How many times do I have to tell you not to run like that! You almost knocked me off my feet!"

"I'm sorry, Mama!" Jacob patted Pepper. "He just likes to run. He has a lot of energy."

"Who does?"

"Pepper, my horse."

Mama grimaced. "Or perhaps *you* have a lot of energy. Let's go make those sandwiches, all right?"

Jacob nodded eagerly, skipping ahead of her into the kitchen and pulling the bread from the cupboard. Daddy was already slicing tomatoes and had lettuce torn up in a bowl.

Mama opened the refrigerator. She fussed around inside for awhile while Jacob dropped bread in the toaster. Finally, she pulled her head out, looking at Daddy in confusion. "Have you been eating the cheese?"

"No." Daddy reached around the door to pull out mayonnaise. "You know I'm not crazy about anything but cheddar."

Mama sniffed. "It's been disappearing for weeks. I thought at first I was imagining it. Jacob." She pinned her gaze on him. "Are *you* eating all the cheese?"

A piece of toast sprang from the toaster into Jacob's hand. "No, Mama. I'm taking it down to Anthony. I don't think he ate the whole time we weren't here—when the Longs weren't here."

Mama's lips pursed. "If you ate the cheese, just say so."

Richard shook his head. "Faith, it's okay. We can get more cheese."

"But if you didn't eat it and I didn't eat it, he's the only one left,"

Mama said, "And he's admitting he took it, but he won't just say he ate it."

"But I didn't, Mama. Anthony did. I won't take anymore if you don't want me to."

Mama's voice got tight. "I don't care if you take cheese. You can *eat,* for God's sake."

Something shot through Jacob's heart at her last words. It hurt and he didn't know why. She said it all the time.

"We can *afford* to feed you, for God's sake!"

There was that twinge of pain again.

"Faith, come on now...."

Mama shook Daddy's hand off her arm but turned on him. "I just want *honesty.* Is it too much to ask for *honesty?*"

"He's just a kid," Daddy said. "Kids have imaginary friends. It's not that big a deal."

Jacob backed away, a piece of toast still in his hand.

Daddy squatted down, holding out his hand. Jacob stayed where he was. Daddy dropped his hand. "Look," he said, "It's okay. I'll get you whatever cheese you like."

"I don't like cheese."

"Okay, I'll get you whatever cheese *Anthony* likes."

"Did you know cheese can be made with milk from lots of animals?" Jacob asked. "Not just cows, but goats and sheep and yaks."

"How do you know that?" Mama's voice fluttered like she was afraid —like the Queen Mother's voice did before Methred went off into battle again. "Do you even know what a yak is?"

Jacob hesitated. Mentioning Anthony upset her.

"How do you know that?" Daddy asked softly.

"Anthony told me," Jacob whispered.

Daddy was silent for a moment. Jacob stared into his eyes—they were brown with golden flecks around the edges. "What kind of cheese does Anthony like?" he asked.

"Richard! Don't encourage...."

Daddy held up a hand. "What kind of cheese does Anthony like?"

"Iberico. It's made with milk from goats, sheep, *and* cows!" His excitement began to come back.

"Richard!"

Daddy fell to his knees and opened his arms and Jacob ran into them. "That's great, Jake. We'll get some Iberico cheese."

"Richard, we do *not* have men living in our walls!"

Jacob felt Daddy's arms around him. He thought of Anthony in the Cellar below and Mama was taking a break to take him to the zoo and she'd be so proud of him that he knew what packy-derms were—she liked him to know things. She might even stop worrying about the cheese, she'd be so proud of him.

And he knew, with the same confidence he felt about the Red Dragon, that all would be well—yes, all would be well.

Jacob ran happily down the path between the polar bears and the sheep.

"Hey, Champ, come on back," Daddy called.

Jacob waited until his parents caught up to him, eating the cotton candy Mama had consented to with a, "Just this once."

"This is the best day ever!" Jacob said, taking Daddy's hand.

"What's your favorite part so far? The rides? The gardens? The animals?"

Jacob half-danced, half-walked beside his father. Como was so much more than a zoo! He'd gone on a pirate ship and a carousel and they'd gone through huge buildings made of glass with millions of trees and flowers and pools and statues and eaten a picnic together across from the bird cage and seen gorillas and tigers and ostriches and a giraffe with a long, thin neck.

"I like it all!" Jacob said. "But where are the pack-derms?"

Mama stopped.

Daddy stopped a step later and he and Jacob looked at Mama.

She tilted her head. "Pachyderms? Do you know what pachyderms are?"

"Elephants." Jacob beamed. "But Mama, why do elephants have two names?"

"How do you know that word?" Mama asked.

"An...." Jacob stopped. "I read it in my book," he whispered.

"I'm glad to hear that," Mama said. But her lips pursed together tightly.

Chapter 12

...the remedy for anger is long-suffering

Gold, silver, steel, iron—all is metal. Gold and silver are cleansed of their dross in the fire; if you gather dross in it, this is against nature. A chalice that was melted and strongly boiled in it, and afterward, through many blows and polishing, was made most beautifully into God's cup— would it, if it could speak curse in cleansing fire and its creators' hands? All this world is God's smithy, to forge his chosen.

– Ancrene Wisse

"Thirty-seven percent of children have imaginary friends by the time they're seven. This is perfectly normal."

Jacob sat outside Mama's office, listening to the man with the round glasses and triangle beard on his chin who spoke from her computer screen. After her zoom call, she was taking him to *eti-kit* lessons, in preparation for the dance on his birthday. He held a stuffed horse, ebony black like Pepper.

Noah, the older boy next door, had given it to him three days ago—the day after Mama and Daddy took him to the zoo. He and the kids had jumped on the trampoline and tossed pennies at the fountain and then all of them had scrambled over the chain link fence and run down to the Ruins.

Jacob gasped at the sight. Stone walls rose into the air with empty windows and no roof. Ivies and flowering vines crawled up the walls— inside and out. It was, for a moment, as if he looked at Dun Aoibhneas, all torn down and broken. Where would Methred and all the others go, if such a thing happened? If the Red Dragon burned it down?

"Hey," Noah said, "It's okay. It was a carriage house. It hasn't been used in a long time and this is a really cool setting."

"Setting?" Jacob asked.

"Yeah—for writing stories or photography. See Amanda Lynn over there?"

Jacob nodded. The big girl who gave them gingerbread was pointing her camera one way and another. "Can we come back here with my brothers in their medieval clothes with their swords?" she asked. "I could take some really cool photographs!"

Jacob nodded, although he had no idea what medieval meant.

"This is just a really cool part of the history of this house from the 1800s," Noah said. "Why does it upset you?"

"It looks like Dun Aoibhneas if it were burned down."

"What's Doon Ahvnis?" Noah sat down beside him, their backs against the ivied walls of the ruins below Jacob's house.

"It's where Methred lives," Jacob said. "And all his court. And his mother the Queen. And we go out to fight the Red Dragon."

"Do you ride horses?" Noah asked.

Jacob nodded eagerly. "I have a black steed named Pepper." But he was thinking about packy-derms.

"I have just the thing!" Noah snapped his fingers. "Hold on." He bolted up and ran. The other kids ran around the ruins, exploring all the walls, and touching the ivy, and scrambling up to windows to peer out.

Noah slid back in beside him, their backs against the wall, and held out the ebony black horse. It lay with its legs stretched out, across Jacob's lap.

"Pretty cool, huh?" Noah said. "I always called him Pepper, too. Coincidence?" He gave an exaggerated wink. "I think not! I think he must be ready to go on to you. I get so busy with school and tests, I don't

have the time for him I should. He doesn't get to stretch his legs like he used to."

Jacob stroked the glossy black mane. "Mama doesn't believe he's real."

"Adults!" Noah snorted. "Pepper and I used to ride all sorts of places after bedtime. Adults forget. Or they never knew."

"But *why* do children have imaginary friends?" Mama demanded. She was upset. Jacob glanced in. She wore her black suit coat with a bright red scarf around her neck. She was pretty, he thought. He was sad he'd upset her. "Children have imaginary friends," she answered her own question, leaning in toward the screen, "because they want to blame their misdeeds on someone else."

"There are many reasons...." the man on the screen said.

"Or because they're unhappy and need to cope with trauma." Mama's voice rose. "So I'm going to have people thinking I'm causing him trauma and a bad mother."

Jacob stroked Pepper's mane. Mama wasn't a bad mother. He wished she didn't think that.

"I am not a bad mother!" Mama said. "I have worked hard—*so hard!* – to give him a *good* life! Everything I've done has been to provide a better life than...."

Jacob's thoughts drifted to the Lovards next door. He did wish Mama would read him stories at night. But she had work emails to answer. Or she needed to relax. *Unwind.*

He sat with Amanda Lynn in the ruins, and she read to him from a book called Black Beauty, *her arm around his shoulder, while her younger brothers and sisters sat around listening.*

When she finished a chapter, the kids ran off.

"You okay, Jacob?" she asked.

He said nothing for a moment. Then he said, "Mama's mad at me."

"I'm sorry." Her arm tightened a little around his shoulder. "Why?"

"Because at the zoo I said the elephants are packy-derms."

"Wow!" Amanda Lynn looked down at him. "That's a fantastic word for a five-year-old! Why is she mad that you knew that?"

Jacob shrugged. His lips tightened a little. His eyes stung. "I don't know. She likes me to know things but she's mad when I do."

"Well, how did you know the word pachyderms?"

"Anthony told me."

"Did you tell your mom that's how you knew it?"

Jacob nodded.

"Hm." Amanda Lynn laid the book in her lap. "I guess your mom hasn't talked to Anthony?"

Jacob shook his head.

"Sometimes people are afraid of what they don't understand."

"But Anthony would never hurt her. He prays for her."

"Of course he wouldn't." Amanda Lynn ruffled his hair and stood up, holding out a hand to him. "Let's come back tomorrow and read some more," she said.

"Mrs. Shorter," said the man on the screen, "nobody who understands childhood imaginary friends will think that. This is perfectly normal and most children know their friends aren't real."

"But he *doesn't!* He believes they *are* real."

Jacob galloped the black horse around the floor outside Mama's office and up over his legs and back again.

"Some children do," the man said. "It's perfectly normal and no harm. In fact, many children with imaginary friends become very socially competent and creative adolescents and it could pave the way for him to be, oh, a great writer."

"He's not becoming a writer. He's going to be a lawyer or a doctor. In the meantime," Mama said, "he's stealing cheese and blaming it on this *Anthony.* I don't like the dishonesty."

"Do you object to him having cheese? Is he maybe afraid of your reaction?"

"He doesn't seem afraid of anything. He can have cheese. I just want the truth."

"In his own mind, it may *be* the truth."

"But it is *not* the truth, and he's lying to me.*"

"Tell me a bit about your own childhood, Mrs. Shorter."

Jacob half-turned to look through the glass doors. He could only see Mama from behind, but her shoulders were scrunched up, the way they were when she had a bad day at work. "This isn't about me," she said.

"Family issues are usually about everyone in the family," the man on the computer screen replied. He rubbed two fingers over his black triangle beard. "Imaginary friends are normal and many families even love telling stories about them." He chuckled. "My niece, when she was three, had story after story about Mrs. Painta, her teacher—who of course didn't exist. Her family found it very amusing and still laughs about it today."

Mama's voice came out tight. "This is *not* amusing! He *thinks there are men living in our walls!*"

Just one, Jacob thought as he pranced Pepper across the floor. And it was a room. It wasn't *exactly* in the walls.

"Have you gone down with him to the basement to show him there's nothing there?"

"No."

That was a good idea, Jacob thought. He could take Mama to the Cellar and she'd see Anthony was real.

"Tell me about your parents," said the man.

"I really don't think this is…"

"Please," said the man. "I'm not talking to Jacob. So I can't do anything about his belief that there's a man in the wall today. But we can talk about your feelings about it, and why you feel that way, which in turn speaks to how *you* decide to deal with it."

"This is just it," Mama said. "I want you to speak to *Jacob.* I want you to convince him there are no men living in our walls!"

"We can set an appointment for that," the man said. "But we have most of your hour left so let's talk about *you* and *your* feelings about this."

"I would rather just make an appointment for Jacob. I can certainly *afford* this appointment, so no concerns about not getting every minute."

Jacob could hear the tension again in her voice. She sounded disapproving of the man. They set a time and date. As they did, Jacob jumped nimbly to his feet and hurried to the kitchen. He tugged at the refrigerator door, then stood on tiptoe to pull open the cheese drawer and peer into it. He saw the package with a big I at the front. He touched each letter. *Iberico*. With a big grin, he grabbed it and turned.

Mama stood there, frowning at him.

"Daddy got Iberico," he said. "You said I can have it."

"Of course you can. Sit down at the table and I'll slice some for you."

"Then can I eat it downstairs?"

"No, we eat food in the kitchen or dining room."

"But I don't...." Jacob stopped. He had been about to say, "I don't like cheese. Daddy got it for Anthony and he's downstairs."

Mama frowned.

At that moment, Daddy walked into the kitchen. "Ah, you found the Iberico! Smart boy! Do you want help cutting it?"

"Well he can't be handling sharp knives himself," Mama said.

Daddy pulled out a cutting board and a knife and swiftly slit the package open. "Faith, I'm sorry to ask; I know you're busy. But could you print up those papers I sent you? My printer is about out of toner." He flashed the knife through the cheese. "And didn't you want to get your nails and hair done today? See if you like that place before you have to get them done for the big party next month?"

"Sure." Mama drew a deep breath. "I'll get those done for you. Yes, you're right about the nails and hair."

She left the room.

Daddy slid the cheese into a small plastic tub and handed it to Jacob with a wink. "Have the cheese anywhere you like. Just make absolutely sure you don't leave any lying around or we'll get mice, okay, Bud?"

Jacob could feel his whole face turn into one big smile. "I won't leave a crumb, Daddy! Thank you!" He jumped on Pepper and galloped out of the kitchen and down the stairs.

In the Garden Room, Jacob knocked at Anthony's window. It immediately slid back. Anthony beamed from behind the bars. "Is that Iberico I smell?"

Jacob danced up and down. "Daddy asked what cheese you like. He got it for you!"

"What an amazing thing!" Anthony reached through the bars, having to slightly tilt the plastic tub to get it through.

"Daddy says don't leave any crumbs or we might have mice."

Anthony was already taking his first bite of cheese. "Mm," he said. "I haven't had Iberico in decades. There will not be a single crumb left! The real danger is that I'll embarrass myself by licking the bowl clean!"

Jacob pulled the stool to Anthony's window and climbed up. "Anthony, why is Mama always so upset with me?"

"Mm." Anthony swallowed a piece of cheese. He heaved a sigh, his eyes on the cross on his wall for a moment, before saying, "Well, your mama isn't upset with *you*. She's upset with other things. But she doesn't know what to do about those things. So she gets upset about what she thinks she *can* do something about."

"Me?"

Anthony nodded.

"But why does anything have to be *done* about me?"

"Well, do you have time for a bit of a story?"

Jacob nodded eagerly.

"Didn't you worry about making friends here?"

Jacob nodded.

"Arren't you still scared about making friends when you start school?"

Jacob nodded.

"Were you ever teased at your old school?"

"There was a boy named Evan who called me names once."

"How did that make you feel?"

"Bad at first," Jacob said. "But Daddy said it wasn't true and Evan must be unhappy so I felt sorry for Evan."

"What if your Daddy said it was true, and Evan was right?"

Jacob scrunched up his face, trying to imagine that.

"Would you feel bad about yourself?" Anthony asked.

"I think so." Jacob nodded vigorously.

"What if your clothes were old and torn and other children teased you about them?"

"Mama says my clothes have to be clean at all times," Jacob said. "She gets upset if I rip the knee of my pants." He felt a small twinge of guilt about the shorts he'd torn climbing the fence. He'd thrown them in the trash, and so far she hadn't noticed they were gone. "Does that have to do with the story?"

"Well," Anthony said, "the story is about a little girl who was very poor. She lived in a trailer home."

"What is that?" Jacob asked.

"It's a long, narrow house, and small inside. Only one floor and only two or three bedrooms."

"We have six," Jacob said. "I think. And a ballroom to dance in."

"And there are only bedrooms and a kitchen and a bathroom."

"Just one?"

"Just one," Anthony confirmed. "There are no offices."

"We have two offices," Jacob said. "One for Mama and one for Daddy."

"This little girl grew up in this very, very small house," Anthony said. "And it was always dirty. Dishes were stacked up. There were empty beer bottles lying around. She was embarrassed to bring friends over because it was dirty."

"Mama wants our house very clean."

"Yes, because she remembers how unpleasant it is to be in a dirty house." Anthony took a bite of the cheese. After a moment he said, "This little girl's clothes were hand-me-downs."

"What is that?"

"Clothes that someone else wore. Maybe two or three or even four other people. Sometimes they were torn or dirty with stains that wouldn't come out. Often, they didn't fit well. Maybe the pants were too short. Or the waist was too big."

"Why?" Jacob tried to imagine someone else having worn his clothes.

He couldn't. They were always his, his alone.

"Because her parents didn't have money for more. So other children teased her about her clothes."

"I knew a girl that kids teased," Jacob said. "She was crying in the hall one day."

Anthony nodded. "Much like this little girl. And she lived like this for many years, until she was older than Amanda Lynn next door. And sometimes—lots of times—her parents told her she deserved to be teased."

"That's mean," Jacob said. "Why did they do that to her?"

"Because *they* were unhappy and angry and they took it out on her, blaming her instead of trying to make their lives better. And she was often very sad."

Jacob tried to imagine Amanda Lynn being sad. Or being teased and made fun of. He couldn't. But it hurt him to think of anyone treating her that way—she was so kind and happy. She should never be teased or made sad.

He tried to imagine Daddy telling him he was bad. He couldn't. Daddy often seemed tired. But he always said *I love you.*

"What happened to the girl?" Jacob asked.

"She decided to do something about it. She decided to never be poor again."

"Poor like too many kids," Jacob asked, "Or poor like not very much money?"

"Not much money. It takes a lot of money to buy a house like you live in."

"Oh." Jacob didn't know what to say.

"It takes a lot of money to have a castle like Methred's."

Jacob's brow furrowed. "Then what do poor people live in?"

"Small houses. Trailer houses. Apartments."

"What's a parment?"

"One floor with only one or two bedrooms, a living room, bathroom, and kitchen. You could fit four apartments on your first floor."

Jacob scrunched his nose. "Does that mean *four* families would live on our first floor!"

Anthony nodded solemnly. "Yes. And several more families on your second floor and two or three on your third floor."

"Mama would *not* like that," Jacob said solemnly. "They would leave messes and be loud when she's on work calls."

"This little girl wanted to live in a big and beautiful house and have beautiful clothes so no one would ever tease her again. So people would think she was as important as those rich girls and be nice to her like everyone was nice to those rich girls. So people would *like* her."

"Did she get that?"

"Well, she got the money." Anthony nodded. "She worked very hard in school to get good grades so she could go to college. She got a very practical degree."

"What's that?"

"Learning to do a job that makes you lots and lots of money."

"Did she earn lots of money?"

Again, Anthony nodded. "She earned lots of money and she met a man who earned lots of money and together they made lots and *lots* of money and she had all the beautiful clothes she wanted and went to expensive restaurants that she could never go to as a child and she had a beautiful, new car instead of her father's rusty truck that embarrassed her and she got the big beautiful house she always wanted."

"As big as ours?" Jacob kicked his feet against the stool in excitement.

Anthony's face broke into a big grin. "*Just* about exactly the same size as yours!"

Jacob clapped his hands. "So she was happy then? Happy like Amanda Lynn? People should be happy!"

Anthony's smile slipped. "No. No, she was not happy."

"Why not?" Jacob's face fell. "She got everything she wanted."

"Because adults seem very old and grown up to you. But the truth is…" Anthony leaned close to the bars, "Most adults are really just children inside. Being a child doesn't feel that long ago to them and many of them—most of them—are still hurt and still afraid."

Jacob tilted his head. He saw for a second in his mind a funny image of Daddy in old-fashioned boys' shorts and Mama in a little girl's dress like he'd seen in picture books. She looked as stressed and angry as she did now.

"Why would she be hurt or afraid if she has all she wanted," Jacob asked.

"Because as a girl, she believed the rich girls were confident and happy. She thought being rich herself would make *her* confident and happy and make people like her. But she got all of that—the money and beautiful clothes and nice house—and found out that inside she's still insecure."

"What does *in skeer* mean?"

"When you're still afraid that you really *are* that ugly, unlikable, poor little girl in dirty clothes your classmates and even sometimes your parents, said you were. When you're afraid that maybe you're a fraud."

"What's that?"

"That you're just pretending to be something you're not."

"Oh." Jacob's eyebrows furrowed for a moment. "Does Mama think *I'm* a fraud? Because she thinks I'm only pretending about Methred."

Anthony put his fingers through the bars. Jacob took them. They were warm. "She doesn't think you're pretending. She thinks you're making it up."

They were silent a moment before Anthony said, "This girl grew up to still be afraid that people would think she was no good. She's still afraid of people not liking her. And she's upset because if the money and clothes and house she thought would make people like her don't make her feel safe—she doesn't know what else to do. She's afraid it's true that no one can ever like her. She's afraid she really is that dirty, ugly girl her classmates and parents said she was."

"That's very sad," Jacob said. "I'm not going to do that."

"Have you watered the plants?" Anthony put the last piece of cheese in his mouth. When Jacob shook his head, he said, "See the watering can over there? Give them a little something to drink so they stay green and beautiful. Not too much, right?"

After tilting the watering can carefully into each of the plants—and there seemed to be a hundred—Jacob came back to his stool.

"There's just a little more to the story," Anthony said. "When that little girl grew up and found that she was still afraid of people not liking her, she tried even harder. She tried to make everything around her perfect. Her house. Her husband. Her son. She thought that if anything and everyone is always perfectly dressed and perfectly clean and has perfect manners and is always well-spoken and is just like what she thought those rich girls were like—then people will like *her*."

"Did it work?" Jacob asked.

"That remains to be seen. But I don't think it will. Happiness is inside us."

"I wish I could help that little girl."

"You can. Pray for her." Anthony tilted the cheese tub sideways between the bars.

"I'm praying for a sister and I still don't have one."

"Sometimes prayer is like fighting a dragon," Anthony said. "Don't you go out and fight that dragon for the sake of other people, knowing you might not come back and you have to do it over and over?"

Jacob nodded.

"Well, sometimes our prayers become much stronger if we know we would give anything for the sake of other people. Just like you will give anything for the sake of the villagers to save them from that dragon."

Jacob didn't know what to say.

Anthony pushed the tub through the bars. "Take that back to your father and assure him there's not even a crumb left."

He smiled and as he did, light seemed to brighten the windows, shining on the thousands of green fronds and leaves. The sad story seemed to fade away—just a story. Jacob hopped off his stool and, waving good-bye to Anthony, galloped back to the kitchen.

Chapter 13

Just as pride is the desire for honor, so also on the contrary, humility is the rejection of honor and love of little praise and of lowliness. This virtue is the mother of all virtues, and gives birth to all of them. ... The clever wrestler takes note of what throw his fellow-wrestler does not know, for with that throw he can cast him down unaware....

– Ancrene Wisse

Summer wore away, with boxes steadily unpacked. Mrs. Channing spent several hours a day in the house, telling Jacob to stand up straight, combing his hair out of his eyes, and teaching him French in addition to the French camp he attended with Miss DuBois. She took him to etiquette lessons and dance lessons while Mama tapped away at her keyboard or dealt with Dan's latest mishap. Jacob didn't understand why she didn't just give him a different job—one he might be good at.

While Mrs. Channing read her magazines in the afternoon, ignoring him, or after she left, Jacob slipped away to play with Joseph and Maria and Elias and Caleb. Amanda Lynn made gingerbread or cookies or cakes and always sent some home with him, that he shared with Anthony. She and Noah and Ethan read stories to him and the younger kids.

News came that he'd been accepted to the Academy. Mama was ecstatic, delighted that his future was a *shurred*. They celebrated with steak tartare at Salut. Mama and Daddy clicked glasses full of cocktails and Mama laughed as if she was really happy.

"I've hired a woman to plan Jacob's birthday party," she said, when the waiter brought their food. "It'll coincide with a party for our new colleagues and the neighbors."

"Wonderful!" Daddy lifted his glass—this one full of wine—and they clinked together across a red-checked table cloth.

"Except the Lovards," Mama said. She wrinkled her nose and said, "Good *God!*"

Jacob kicked his feet against the rail on his chair. He knew Anthony would bow his head and look sad at the way she had just used God's name.

"What if they expect to bring that rag-tag bunch of kids to a civilized event and embarrass me in front of my colleagues?"

"What's rag tag?" Jacob poked at the tartare with his fork.

"Low class." Mama blew a little air out her nose and lifted her glass of white wine to her mouth.

"What's low class? Is that like...kindergarten?" He was going into first grade. "Cause Amanda Lynn's really old. I think she's like in fifteenth grade."

Daddy laughed. "No. Low class is like people who wear old, dirty clothes or drive...." he glanced at Mama. "Rusty old...cars. Or use vulgar language."

"What's vulgar language?"

"Like swearing. Bad words."

Jacob stared at Mama, his eyebrows drawn together. "Isn't saying *God* swearing?"

Mama put her fork down on her plate. "Ex-*cuse* me? Did you just say I'm low class?"

Jacob's lip trembled. "No, Mama."

"Faith, he didn't...."

Mama drew a deep, shuddering breath. "Jacob, I will not be insulted by my own son. I am not low class and I do not use vulgar language."

Jacob felt tears sting at his eyes. He blinked fiercely. "I didn't mean that, Mama. I only wanted to understand."

Thy will be done! The walls seemed to speak. And suddenly Methred seemed to be beside him. And he could almost feel Methred watching him, asking Anthony's question: *How much are you willing to give up to help someone else?*

Anthony's story about the little girl sprang to mind. But it quickly disappeared with other thoughts. He didn't want to anger Mama. But he looked up. "But Mama, they're not low class. Their clothes are very clean and their house is very clean and they never, ever use vulgar language. And they pray."

Mama pulled a long, slow breath in through her nose and drew herself up very straight. "You've been in their house?"

Jacob nodded.

"When did this happen?"

"When you were working. They invited me and Amanda Lynn gave me gingerbread and Noah reads me stories and we jump on the trampoline. And they never use bad words."

"They breed like rabbits over there. I will not have feral children making me look bad in front of my colleagues. The discussion is over, Jacob. My colleagues will be bringing their children and it's important for you to know them. You have a very bright future, knowing the right people. I assume you're paying attention in your etiquette lessons? Eat your steak tartare."

Jacob stood up straight at his etiquette lessons and said please and thank you and learned which fork to use when and learned the V-kneed waltz at his dance lessons. Mama bought him new school clothes—dress shirts and dark blue suit coats and ties with crests on them and dark blue shorts and pants—and told him how fortunate he was to be admitted to the Academy.

He brought Anthony cheese after Mrs. Mole left and before Mama called him up for dinner and Anthony told him stories of Mid-Evil Europe and knights and kings and saints he had known and Jacob heard more stories from Noah, and when they talked about Malachi, and he asked, they said, "Malachi is sick. He's sleeping. Maybe tomorrow." And Amanda Lynn gave him gingerbread to take home and held his hand and said, "You're asking Anthony to pray for us?"

And Jacob sank into bed exhausted at night, staring at the consolations on his ceiling. Listening to Mrs. Lovard read stories through the open windows, he fell asleep.

Methred led his men silently under the moonlight, while Jacob stayed with a small contingent, lighting numerous campfires, across the lea before the Red Dragon's cave. They spread out, stretched thin across the false camp, banging on drums and clanging spears and swords on targes, their small round shields.

They paraded horses in circles before the tents, holding torches high, trying to fool the old beast and keep his attention from possibly catching the bulk of the army moving into position above his lair.

Jacob rode the longest of all. He made the most noise. He wanted his men home with their wives and children. They had lost too many already.

Of course, he knew the Red Dragon might well fly out and attack them in the morning. Perhaps none of them would survive the way he swooped in, breathing fire that seared tents and snatched up horses or men in its claws.

But if they kept his attention diverted, then Methred had a chance of laying the trap, of rolling the stones down and sealing the Red Menace away where it could do no harm ever again.

Finally, Jacob let his tired steed stop. He sat atop it, staring up at the north sky. The Plough winked there. The Big Dipper. In another life, it might have been called that. Below it, low on the horizon, was Cassiopeia, and between them, the Northern Star.

He threw his leg over his horse's back and landed on the ground. Soon, the horse was fed and cared for, and Sir Jacob himself was under his covers in his tent.

A great roar awoke him with the sun still below the horizon, barely lighting the sky to gray. He bolted from his tent, scrambling to grab at his armor and shouting for his page.

Outside his tent, he could see across the wide lea, with mist rising up off it, to boulders and stones and branches and even logs rolling down the distant hill, spilling over the edge and one by one blocking the entrance to the Dragon's cave.

But the entrance was large.

Fire and smoke billowed out suddenly over the boulders piling up there, a brilliant flash of orange against the gray of pre-dawn.

"Faster, faster!" Jacob whispered urgently, as his page helped him into his armor. But the stones could only fall so fast. Around him, his small remnant army flew to don their armor and snatch up their swords and bows.

The Red Dragon appeared in the gaping maw of the cave, shaking its scaled head in anger.

"Faster!" Jacob shouted to his own men, and with his armor strapped on, he vaulted up onto his horse. "Archers! Ride!"

The Red Dragon pushed its head out over the growing berm. A huge rock rolled down, glancing off his red-scaled head. He roared, shooting out a stream of fire. One of Methred's men fell, screaming. The Dragon pushed out, knocking rocks and logs out of the way. It stretched its huge wings, a fearsome sight. Jacob's heart flipped over. They had failed!

Just then, a boulder nearly as big as a man rolled over the cliff, striking one of the massive wings. The Red Dragon screamed in pain.

"Ride!" Jacob shouted. He charged forward, his sword drawn. His archers rode beside him, clutching horses with knees as they nocked arrows into bows.

The Dragon pushed awkwardly over the debris before its cave, and stumbled into a stilted run, its wings stretched. One last log rolled over the cliff, catching it on the tail. It thrashed its scaly tail, spread its wings, and ran at Jacob and his men. His archers, cool as always, let loose a volley of arrows, a thick cloud flying across the misty lea. The Dragon screamed again as it lifted into awkward flight. Several arrows hit home, striking wings and breast.

They were pebbles to the mighty beast.

Jacob couldn't help but admire its strength and majesty as it soared into the air, despite its crippled wing and wounded tail and half a dozen arrows in its wings and body.

His archers shot more arrows straight up as it soared over them, a great black shadow in the gray morning sky. It screeched, blowing down fire as it passed and he heard the scream of one of his men.

His heart sank. They had failed.

Sorcho, the oldest archer, rode up beside him. They watched silently for a moment as the Dragon sailed away into the east, where the sun showed its first rays. Mist curled around their horses' knees, and up to their noses.

"It's the best we've ever done," Sorcho said. "He's wounded."

"The goal was to stop him," Sir Jacob grated out. "Instead, one of Methred's men has fallen and one of ours is injured. Perhaps badly."

"Sir Jacob," Sorcho replied, his bow hanging at his horse's side, "There is always a price to be paid in fighting evil. Two men have paid it today. Perhaps tomorrow it will be you or me and we will gladly pay it to protect our people. But we are a day closer to ending the tyranny this Red Dragon has held over us these many years."

Jacob stared at the ground, swirling with mist that reached to his toes in the stirrups. Yes, they were closer. But men were still injured.

Chapter 14

They are better [of] whom the apostle...says "You are dead and your life is hidden with Christ. When he who is your life appears again and breaks forth like the daylight after night's darkness, you also will break forth with him, brighter than the sun, into eternal joy." Those who are dead in this way now live a higher life.... This is a blessed death which makes a living man or a living woman like this, away from the world.

– Ancrene Wisse

"How was your first day of school!" Jacob ran to the fence that separated him from Elias, Maria, and Joseph. First grade had not been so daunting as he feared, despite the dark blue shorts and jacket with some kind of embroidered patch on it. They'd told their names and a little about themselves and the other kids at the Academy had seemed very interested in the Red Dragon and his move from California, and Anthony.

Elias leaned on the fence, a penny in his hand. He flung it at the fountain, missing by a long way. "We do school all year."

"What!" *Those poor kids*, Jacob thought. "Don't you ever get a break?"

"Why would we want one?" Maria asked. "Learning is fun."

"But learning is different from school." Jacob hoisted himself over the fence. "I learn from Anthony and Mama and Methred. But school is different. Don't you like to be away from school?"

Maria shook her head. "Learning is what school *should* be. We're learning all the time. Like, watch how Elias throws this next penny. It's about force and velocity."

Jacob watched as Elias set his wrist, another penny in hand. He had no idea what *vlocity* was.

"Force," Maria told him.

Elias narrowed his eyes, took a deep breath, and snapped his wrist. The penny sailed to the edge of the fountain, clipping the inner stone as the boulders had clipped the Red Dragon's wing, and bounced in. Maria and Joseph cheered, and Elias grinned.

"Where do you go to school?" Jacob asked.

"We home school," Maria said.

Jacob scrunched his nose. "Where's that?"

Joseph laughed. "At *home*. We learn *at home*."

"We don't go to a school," Elias said. "Our mom teaches us and sometimes our dad."

Jacob tried to process that. "You don't go to school? Everyone goes to school." Mama told him over and over, school was important for the future. "Don't you want a good job?"

Maria laughed. "We *do* go to school. We go to school in our dining room."

Jacob thought about the children at Dun Aoibhneas. They learned from their mothers, the older pages and squires, the smiths in the forges, the cooks in the kitchen. They didn't attend a school. But they learned. Maybe it wasn't so strange.

Amanda Lynn appeared on the back porch. "Are you coming in for apple crisp, Jacob?" she asked.

Mama was in a work meeting on zoom. Daddy was downtown. Mrs. Channing would be there mostly on Saturdays and some evenings now that school had started—but not tonight. Jacob nodded eagerly and ran with Maria, Jacob, and Elias up the back stairs and into the dining room. The other kids burst from all corners of the house to grab chairs around the big dining room table. Even Noah and Ethan left their desks this time and came to the table. The kids all did the squiggly thing over their foreheads and shoulders and chests again and then dug into the apple crisp joyfully.

"Knock, knock!" shouted Levi.

"Who's there!" all the kids answered with glee.

Jacob took a big bite of the apple crisp. It was delicious!

"Rita!"

"Rita Who?" all the kids shouted.

"Rita Good Book Today!"

All the Lovard kids laughed. Noah told another joke. And Maria another. And Noah another.

"How was your first day of school?" Amanda Lynn asked as she set down the last plate.

Jacob realized she was talking to him. He swallowed his apple crisp. "Good. I'm very lucky to get into the Academy. Mama says my future is a *shurred* if I study and do well."

The Lovard kids were quiet for a moment. Then Amanda Lynn put a hand on his shoulder. "That's wonderful. Were the kids nice?"

Jacob nodded. And a thought occurred to him. "Anthony is praying for you—like you asked me to. Is it about Malachi?"

The Lovard kids suddenly got silent. They looked at their plates. Their forks stopped.

Jacob looked from one to the other. "He's the only one I haven't met," he said. "I asked Anthony to pray and he said he does. I prayed, too."

He looked from one to the other. They stared at their plates.

Amanda Lynn sat down beside him. "Malachi is very sick. He went to the hospital today."

An image flashed before Jacob, of Methred's man falling off the cliff. "Is he going to die?" he asked. He wondered if he did—would he know it? Or would he be a ghost thinking he was still alive?

Amanda Lynn stared at her hands in her lap. "If he does, he'll be with God in Heaven."

Jacob looked at her hands, clenched in her lap. He thought about Methred's man and all the others who had died fighting the Red Dragon. Where was Heaven exactly? Anthony said the sky but Jacob couldn't see it. Didn't Methred's monks and priests speak of such things? He had never really thought much about it. He had only thought of their families left behind.

Anthony's question came to him again: *What would he do for the sake of others?* He jumped up, pushing his chair back from the table. "Some saints can heal. Anthony said if someone's really sick, we'll find out if he can. I'm going down to Anthony right now. He'll pray really hard and Malachi will get better."

Amanda Lynn smiled, taking his hand in hers. "Thank you, Jacob."

"Hey, Jake." Noah put a hand on his shoulder as he started past Noah's chair. "God always answers prayers. We believe that. But sometimes the answer is No."

Jacob was silent a moment. Then he asked, "Why do we pray, then?"

"Lots of reasons," Maria said.

"Prayer changes *us*," Amanda Lynn said. "And helps us face whatever we have to face in life."

"Because God *does* listen to prayers," Noah said. "He cares about us. And sometimes prayers stop a terrible thing or make the difference in something really good coming along."

"But sometimes," Ethan said, "there's a reason something *has* to happen. Even though it's a bad thing, it might be what leads to better things."

"Like what?" Jacob asked.

"Like Malachi's doctor," said Levi. All eyes turned to him.

"What about him?" Amanda Lynn asked.

"His little sister died when she was five. It's what made him want to become a doctor instead of a composer. He said all he ever wanted to do growing up was write music. It's all he ever did. And then she died and it's what made him study so hard and why he does research now, even on his own time. He's learned ways to help kids that we wouldn't know except for him."

"So now hundreds of kids have lived because of him," Maria said.

"And Malachi will, too!" Jacob ran from the room. "I need to talk to Anthony."

Jacob climbed the back steps and ran across the wide hall between the front and back doors, heading for the stairs. "Whoa," Mama said, coming out of her office. "Where've you been?"

"With the Lovards next door."

Mama frowned. "I told you I don't want you playing there."

"Can they come here?"

Mama sniffed. "There's not room for all of them. I need it quiet. I told you they're not proper playmates."

Daddy appeared at the rail upstairs. "Hey, Champ! How was school?"

Jacob ran up the stairs, hugging his father. "It was good. Do you know the kids next door do school in their own house and they *like* school? Their mom and dad teach them fun stuff."

"Hey, cool," Daddy said. "Should we go have some cheese?"

"Don't encourage him with that nonsense," Mama called up.

"I don't like cheese," Jacob said at the same time. But he said it softly, hoping Mama wouldn't hear.

Daddy leaned down saying equally softly, "How about I give you an apple and a piece of cheese for Anthony?"

Jacob nodded eagerly, while Mama marched to the bottom of the stairs saying, "Richard, do *not* encourage that nonsense."

Daddy took Jacob's hand, and they came down the stairs. "Faith, it's harmless. Do you want to join us for a snack?"

Mama rolled her eyes. "I have work to do."

"Faith, come on. Five minutes. You need to eat well."

Mama narrowed her eyes. She gave a slow nod of her chin, indicating Jacob, and looked back at Daddy. "We've talked about this, Richard."

"Nothing's set in stone, Faith. Come on, I'll make you that sandwich you used to love with lettuce and tomatoes and spam."

"Low class, Richard. I never loved that."

"I'll cut you an apple and cover it with peanut butter." Daddy beamed. Jacob wondered what was up. He seemed unusually happy.

"Five minutes," Mama said and swung through the big square hall into the kitchen.

She seated herself at the table, watching as Daddy sliced apples into four and smeared them with peanut butter. "Remember when we used to have apples and peanut butter on our picnics?" He grinned at her.

Mama's shoulders relaxed a little bit. She had a small smile. The afternoon light glinted off the little garnet earrings in her ears.

"We should all go have a picnic in the ruins," Daddy said.

Mama sighed. "Maybe when I'm done with work—maybe on Saturday."

Jacob kicked his legs under his chair, watching as Mama ate her apples. For a few minutes, she looked happier. Then she pushed her dark hair back and stood up with a sigh. "I have to get back to these reports."

Saturday wold be full of reports, too, Jacob thought.

Daddy smiled. "It was nice to have five minutes with you." He opened the refrigerator and reached for the cheese drawer.

"Richard!" Mama stood up. "Do *not* encourage him in this fantasy. I mean it!"

Daddy shut the door.

"You know you're spending way too much money on cheese. You have to stop that."

"Yes, dear."

"Don't *yes, dear* me. I mean it."

Daddy's grin grew. "Yes, dear."

"No more cheese!" Mama huffed and turned on her heel.

As soon as she left the room, Daddy opened the refrigerator again and handed Jacob a block of Gouda cheese. He winked. Jacob laughed, swung his right leg up over his steed, and threw himself high in the saddle. He galloped away to the stairs, going quietly past Mama's office.

In the Garden Room, Jacob jumped off Pepper. Anthony's door was sliding back before he could knock.

"Hello, Saint in the Cellar!" Jacob said. "Daddy says this is gooey. Do you like gooey?"

Anthony looked at the cheese, holding it up to the sunlight pouring into his cell from the Garden Room. "I think that's called *goo-duh*. G—O—U—D—A."

"I call it Badda," Jacob said. "I hate cheese."

"More for me!" Anthony grinned and took a bite.

Jacob hopped up on the stool that now stayed by Anthony's window. "Anthony? Mama always needs to be the boss of everything. We always need to do everything she says. Even daddy."

"Mm." Anthony swallowed the cheese. "Is it getting frustrating?"

Jacob nodded. "It's not fair."

"It's always good to know why people do what they do. Sometimes that helps us have compassion."

"What's that?"

"Caring for people, loving them, maybe even feeling a little sad for them because we know they're hurting."

"I don't think Mama hurts. Not as long as we do what she says."

Anthony scooted his chair a bit closer to the grate. "What if it was a lot worse?" he asked. "What if every part of your life was controlled by her?"

"But it *is!* She even says Daddy can't buy you cheese now."

"Try to imagine worse," Anthony said. "What if she drank too much wine and yelled all day every day and shouted at you to do chores and then found fault with all the chores you did? What if she spent all the money, over and over again, so there was nothing left for food and you had nothing to eat some days?"

Jacob tried to imagine

"What if your house was so dirty you didn't want to bring friends home and your Mama and Daddy wore filthy clothes and smoked and drank and kids at school made fun of them?"

"The kids at my school thought Mama was very pretty," Jacob said.

"How would you feel if they said mean things and you were hungry many days?" Anthony asked. "And there was nothing you could do about it?"

"Really bad."

"Would you feel like your life was completely out of your control? Like you were completely at someone else's mercy?"

Jacob nodded.

"Would you want to try to have control over your own life?"

Jacob nodded again.

"That's why she does it," Anthony said. "Her father was a tyrant." Before Jacob could ask, Anthony added, "A tyrant is like the Red Dragon —someone who does anything they want to other people, no matter who it hurts. A tyrant only cares about himself."

"Oh."

"So when your mother was very young, she promised herself nobody would ever have that much power and control over her again."

Jacob's brow furrowed. "But me and Daddy don't have *any* control. We're not allowed to do anything."

"No, because she's afraid if she lets go even a little, maybe she'll be back where she was, with no say over her own life, with your dad drinking and yelling and spending all the money so there's none left for food."

"But Daddy wouldn't do that. He says we always save some. He showed me one day. So we wouldn't have to worry about a rainy day, he said." He didn't know why things cost more in the rain.

"Yes, your father is a good man," Anthony agreed. "But sometimes when people grow up, they believe the whole world and everyone in it is what they knew when they were children. She doesn't *know* your father wouldn't do that to her."

"Oh." Jacob kicked his feet back and forth, thinking about that. Suddenly he sat up straighter, hope in his eyes. "I could *tell* her he won't!"

"You could." A little bit of the candlelight in Anthony's cell glinted off the bald part of his head. "But you have to understand, if you do tell her, it won't convince her. Because she doesn't believe it with her head. She believes it with her heart." He tapped his chest. "Where she doesn't even realize she believes it. And changing what someone believes in their heart takes a lot more than just telling them it isn't true."

There was a moment's silence before Anthony added, "Your mother is, in her heart, a scared little girl trying to have some control over her own life. You should pray for her."

Jacob nodded. "I will. But I pray every night for a sister and I still don't have one."

Anthony winked. "Maybe you do and you just haven't seen her yet."

Jacob frowned. "There are a lot of rooms in this house." Suddenly, he smiled broadly. "I'm going to go look!" He jumped off his chair and leapt up on Pepper. Then he stopped and looked back.

"Anthony, I forgot. I came down to tell you Malachi is very sick. He's at the hospital. You'll pray for him?"

"Of course."

Jacob smiled and galloped down the paneled hall along the crimson carpet between the glowing sconces and up the stairs. Babies were small. He might have to look very carefully. Hope filled his heart.

"Jacob!" As he reached the top of the stairs, Mama's voice cut through his thoughts. She looked sternly out from her office. "I'm on a zoom meeting. Will you *please* keep it down."

Jacob stared at her. She didn't look like a scared little girl. She looked like an annoyed mother who might send him to his room. Then suddenly, for just a moment, he thought he saw what Anthony was talking about.

He trotted Pepper more quietly up the wide stairs leading up to the second floor. Pepper seemed to understand, even tiptoeing on the carpet runner while Jacob held the heavy wood banister.

At the top, Daddy waved from his office.

Jacob waved back and then they galloped again, going from room to room, opening drawers and looking under beds. They raced up to the third floor, searching the bedrooms there and the ballroom and the kitchen, even opening cupboards.

He was only a little disappointed to find no baby sister. Anthony had only said maybe. He went to his room and prayed for a sister and for

Malachi, before climbing up on the chair at his desk and starting his homework. *What did you do this summer?*

I moov to a new hose and fownd a sant in my seller.

Jacob sat by the window each night, with a blanket pulled up around his shoulders. It was cool at night now, cooler than California ever got except maybe in January. The kids waved at him and he waved back. Mrs. Lovard smiled at him and began reading about four children named Peter, Susan, Edmund, and Lucy who were sent to London during the war because of air raids.

Jacob leaned his head against the cool glass, drifting into a story of an old professor and his housekeeper Mrs. Macready in a big house that you never seemed to find the end of, a house full of unexpected places. He imagined it must look quite a bit like his house. And finally, Lucy found a wonderful world inside a wardrobe. Since it was full of coats, Jacob thought a wardrobe must be a closet.

He thought about all Anthony had said about Mama.

He thought about Mama calling the Lovards low class.

He listened to Mrs. Lovard read, and pulled another blanket up around him. He propped pillows by the window sill and curled up in the cool night, listening to sound of the children running through the house, exploring and playing.

Father Antoine greeted the men home. A feast awaited them. Minstrels sang. Methred's mother, the queen mother, put a chain of gold around Jacob's neck. The lute lilted and the minstrels sang of Brave Sir Jacob fighting the Red Dragon and his brilliant plan.

A huge roasted pig sat on a table in the center of the great hall with an apple in its mouth and smoke billowing out its nose. Garlands of greens and parsnips and onions and every sort of bread and vegetable surrounded it in a beautiful array.

Jacob wanted to flee to his chambers. They'd lost one man and another was injured. He didn't deserve a gold chain. But he could not offend the queen mother by refusing.

Methred beamed at him, beckoning him to the head table. "Well done, Sir Jacob!"

Jacob gave a bow to his friend and sat. A trumpet blew. There were speeches hailing Jacob's near-conquest. Hope danced in the air. Finally, wounded now, the dragon would be vanquished!

Jacob supposed it was true.

Methred drank wine and toasted him, lifting his chalice high.

The maidens danced, the minstrels played, the night wore on.

"You are not joyful, my friend," Methred said at last.

"No," Jacob said. "Arbella mourns the loss of her husband tonight; her children mourn the loss of their father, while we drink and make merry. I would prefer to be...." The image of a chapel flashed before his mind. "I would prefer to be anywhere but here. Perhaps in the chapel at her side. So she knows someone cares."

Methred was silent for a long time. He took a draught of his wine and set the chalice down beside his half-eaten chicken leg. "Did I ever tell you about the time I met Anthony of Padua?" he asked.

Jacob shook his head. "Who's he?"

"The great saint, canonized by Pope Gregory IX himself. Do you know what inspired him to move from the Augustinians to the Franciscans?"

"I know nothing of him at all."

"He was born to wealthy parents. His father, Count Martin, owned a great manor that produced hundreds of acres of crops." Methred stared at the candles burning in the large chandelier high above, and smiled. "My father traveled there once. He knew Anthony when he was a child—when he was still called Fernando."

Jacob twirled the stem of his chalice between his fingers.

Methred chuckled. "His father Martin had a man in his employ—perhaps the best cheese maker ever!"

Jacob frowned. "Cheese?"

"My father brought some home. The best cheese I've ever had!"

"Hm." Jacob watched the minstrels play.

"I'm a knight," Methred said. "I'm no saint like Anthony. But we—knights and saints—are the same in one way."

"What is that?" Jacob turned to him.

"I heard one of his last sermons. I was quite young. It inspired me and I learned all I could of him. He was in the Augustinians when the five Franciscan martyrs were brought home from Morocco."

Jacob waited. A reed flute joined the lute. The dancing maidens placed their right hands one on top of another and moved in a circle like spokes on a wheel.

"They were beheaded there for preaching Christ. Their remains were brought to Anthony's monastery in a solemn ceremony, attended by the queen. It became Anthony's greatest desire to die for the sake of others, to bring the faith to others."

When Jacob said nothing, Methred added, "To die for the sake of others—Jacob, this is what we do." He leaned forward speaking earnestly. "We offer our lives to protect the people of this castle and the people of our villages. Sir Rolund *knew* this. We all know this."

"Yes," Jacob said. "And Arbella still grieves while we sing and feast."

Methred placed a hand on Jacob's shoulder. "She is in the chapel even now, keeping vigil over him. Go to her. But know that she and her children will be well-cared for. Rolund has not died in vain and soon, our villagers as well as his own children, will be safe from this Red Dragon because of him and all those who risk their lives repeatedly."

Jacob stared at the pig.

Methred put a hand on his shoulder. "What father," he asked, "what parent, would not give their own life to protect their child? It is what parents do and it is what Rolund has done."

Jacob rose, giving a bow to Methred. He disappeared through the small door behind the head table, going up the narrow twisting stone stairs, between rows of torches, flickering flame-light on the stone walls.

"Sir Jacob."

Jacob stopped.

Father Antoine stood before him. "A moment of your time?"

"Of course," Jacob said.

"You didn't watch the Wolf," the priest said. "You think it is a small thing. But it is the key. You must watch *the Wolf,* not the Dragon."

"I'm sorry, Father," Jacob said. He felt the weight of his failure to heed the priest's words.

"The consequences will be dire if you do not stop the *wolf.*"

He disappeared. He just seemed to melt away into the wall.

Jacob was not sure how he did it. He didn't care. He opened the big wooden door to the chapel. Sir Rolund lay on a raised bier before the altar, in full armor but for the helmet that sat on the floor before the bier; his sword in his hands. His long dark hair had been smoothed back. He had been a happy father, laughing with his children, hugging them and spending time with them.

The widow Arbella knelt there in black, a long black veil falling down her back. Five children knelt on either side of her. Their sniffles came now and again. The youngest would be with a nurse.

Arbella turned at the sound of the door. Her eyes met Jacob's.

He stepped forward and offered his hand. She took it. Jacob bowed for just a moment over her fingertips, before lifting his eyes to hers. "He was a great man. I'm very sorry."

She drew her kerchief quickly under her nose. "He is in Heaven with God. He gave his life for the sake of others and such a man goes directly to Heaven. We pray for those left behind." She smiled a bit, then bowed her head again.

Jacob went to the pew opposite hers and knelt there. *Prayer.*

He wondered why he didn't remember praying here before.

Prayer is talking to invisible friends in the sky.

But God was invisible and somewhere up there. And Rolund was certainly in His wonderful mansions, laughing as he had always done on earth.

Jacob felt a strong sense of peace in the chapel.

He bowed his head. *I don't know You. I don't understand. But I feel You here. I ask for peace and all good things for Arbella and her children.*

He lifted his eyes to the Crucifix and frowned.

What did Father Antoine mean about the Wolf?

Chapter 15

Those who don't know they're sick seek no help. To such as her the angel in the Apocalypse speaks: You say you have no need of medicine, but you are blind of heart and do not see how you are poor and naked of holiness and spiritually wretched.

– Ancrene Wisse

Mama picked him up from his dance lesson. She wore a light, red cardigan that almost reached her knees and matched her red nail polish and looked so pretty against her dark hair, Jacob thought. "What dance did you work on today?" she asked, taking his hand. Colorful red and orange and gold leaves swirled around his feet as they crossed the sidewalk.

"The V-Knees Waltz."

They learned a new one each week. This was the fourth.

"Vi-*en*-nese." She opened the back door of the car to let him in, and sliding into her own seat a moment later, said, "Are you remembering to use good posture?"

"Yes, Mama." He pulled at his tie, wanting it off. "VN Knees." He couldn't wait to talk to Anthony and jump on the Lovard kids' trampoline. Or maybe Amanda Lynn would sit in the ruins and tell him more about Narnia. Listening across even the small distance between the houses, he didn't always catch all of it.

"Could you read *Narnia* to me?" he asked.

"Hm?" Mama glanced over her shoulder. "You know I relax after dinner."

"But maybe sometimes...."

"I've given you lots of wonderful books and you know how to read for yourself."

Jacob stared out his window, saying nothing.

"Jacob, really, it's a very little thing—I just need a little peace and quiet after I've worked all day."

"Yes, Mama." He watched out the window at the cars passing by, and city streets. "Mama, what are air raids?"

"Air raids?" Once again she glanced back at him. "What do you mean?"

"The air raids in London." He knew about London. He'd been there with Methred. It had been big, full of life and color.

"Did you learn about that in school?" She sounded surprised.

"No. In the Narnia books."

"What are those?"

"Just books." He didn't want to tell her about listening to stories with the Lovards at night.

"Those were during World War Two," she said. "German planes flew over the city of London shooting and dropping bombs."

"Did they turn it into ruins?" He hated to think of London in ruins.

"You don't need to worry about that ever happening. It was a long time ago." Mama pulled into a parking ramp. "I'm surprised you know about that."

"Aren't we going home?" Jacob asked.

Mama was already out of the car, rounding it and opening his door. "You have an appointment with Dr. Wilson." In seconds, Jacob was almost running to keep up with her as her red heels *tap-tapped* across the parking ramp and she aimed the key fob over her shoulder, beeping the car's locks. "We're on a tight schedule."

"I'm not sick. I don't need a doctor," Jacob protested.

"Just to talk." Mama led him into a maze of hallways and up an elevator and down another hall and after a short wait in a room with toys, which he didn't touch, a tall man with a narrow face and straight, black hair that fell oddly in his eyes, and a little triangular beard, welcomed them into his room.

Jacob recognized him from the zoom meeting. He wanted to turn and run. But he couldn't help looking around the room in wonder. One wall was painted sky-blue with clouds up near the ceiling and flowers near the floor. A play house with pink walls and white shutters stood against it.

Another wall was painted forest green, full of fir trees. A gray plastic castle, big enough to climb into, with a second floor and a slide coming down from the parapets stood against that wall.

A third wall held a long, low desk with child-sized chairs. There were low shelves full of toys of every kind.

The tall man held out a hand. "I'm Dr. Wilson. You can call me Dave."

"How do you do, Dr. Wilson?" Jacob shook his hand as he'd been taught.

"Anything you'd like to play with, Jacob, feel free," Dr. Wilson said.

"Aren't you going to talk with him?" Mama seated herself in a chair, a big red chair with a rounded upholstered back that almost matched the color of her heels and cardigan.

"I'd like to go over a few things with you first," Dr. Wilson said. "Jacob, anything you'd like to play with. I think you like castles?"

Jacob nodded. He looked at Mama, questioning.

"Mrs. Shorter," Dr. Wilson said, "to be blunt, you asked me to help him. Please let me do my job the way I've found works best."

"Go ahead, Jacob." Mama's lips pursed. She stared at Dr. Wilson.

Jacob went to the castle, crawling in underneath first. Inside was a collection of toy knights. Mama's voice sounded far off, murmuring with Dr. Wilson. Jacob tipped one of the knights over, laying it on its back. Rolund was in heaven, Arbella said. Anthony said heaven was full of mansions.

There was really nothing to do in the castle. He wanted to be with the Lovard kids, jumping on a trampoline or eating gingerbread or listening to stories. He crawled out, and climbed up to the second story. There, in the corner, sat a big red dragon, a stuffed toy. Jacob picked it up, flying it around over the castle. He bent one wing down, and it wobbled, flying poorly.

"You found the red dragon," Dr. Wilson said. "Do you like dragons?"

Jacob shook his head.

Mama stared at him. She twisted her ring, the ruby one on her right hand, not the wedding ring.

Dr. Wilson rose from his chair near Mama and came over to the castle, squatting down. "Does he have a name?"

Jacob shook his head.

"Tell him if he has a name," Mama said. "Tell him about Methelred."

"Mrs. Shorter, it's often better if parents wait outside."

"He is my son. I want to know that you're helping him."

"Mrs. Shorter." Dr. Wilson stood up, facing her. "I think that perhaps he won't talk if you're here."

"Are you suggesting my own son is afraid of me!" Mama stood up on her red heels. "I am offended."

Dr. Wilson approached her, speaking softly. Mama huffed and turned on her red heels and left. Dr. Wilson sat awhile. He smiled at Jacob.

"Why are you playing with the dragon if you don't like dragons?" he finally asked.

Jacob glanced at the door Mama had disappeared through. He shrugged. "Dragons can hurt people."

"Which people has the dragon hurt?"

"Children."

"We want to protect those children."

"How does a knight fight something as powerful as a dragon?"

"Are you comfortable in the dress shirt and tie?"

Jacob shrugged.

"You can take the tie off if you'd be more comfortable."

Jacob took it off, laying it neatly atop the castle parapets.

"Knights fight powerful things just like we all do sometimes," Dr. Wilson said. "They think it through and study the situation." He tapped his head. "Intelligence. Know your enemy. Know the situation. Everything—the big and the small."

Jacob set the red dragon down in a corner of the castle, and climbed down the front. He sat in the red chair Mama had left. Dr. Wilson's words made him think of Father Antoine's: *You didn't watch the wolf.* "How do you know the sitch-ation with a dragon?" he asked.

Dr. Wilson raised an eyebrow. "That is a very good question. What does the dragon want? Why does it do what it does?"

"Because it's hungry?" Jacob thought of Anthony eating cheese. The Red Dragon ate knights and children. *What do we hunger and thirst for?* He thought of Anthony talking about Mama and the things she feared and wanted.

"Yes, I suppose a dragon would be hungry," Dr. Wilson said.

"But what if it's hungry, but you just can't let it keep eating the children in the village?"

"Hm." Dr. Wilson let out a heavy breath. "That is a very difficult problem. Because hunger is a funny thing. Sometimes people—and probably dragons, too—eat for reasons that have nothing to do with hunger."

"Why else would you eat?"

"Because you're bored. Or lonely. Or sad." Dr. Wilson tapped the side of his head again. "The mind does funny things to us. Many people are embarrassed to admit they're lonely or sad. They're 'hungry' for someone to love them or hungry for company. So they tell themselves they're hungry for food. And they eat. So they don't have to admit to themselves that they're afraid no one wants to love them or be their friend."

Anthony had talked about Mama feeling like a small child, feeling like no one would like her.

"So what if a dragon is eating the village's children because it's lonely or sad?" Jacob got up off the chair Mama had sat in and went back to the castle. He stood on tiptoe to pull the red dragon from its place and bring it back to Dr. Wilson. "It can't just keep eating children."

"No. It definitely can't." Dr. Wilson smiled. They stared at each other for a moment. "*Was* the dragon eating children?" Dr. Wilson asked.

"Yes. And the Wolf, too. It was about to get a little boy when I saved him."

"That was very brave."

"But the Red Dragon is bigger and we can't seem to stop it."

"You were able to protect the boy from the Wolf. Maybe you should start there."

"I think Anthony would agree with you."

"Who is Anthony?" Dr. Wilson asked.

Jacob stared at the man. Mama thought he was lying. "Can I go now?" he asked.

"Of course."

"Mama will be mad if I leave now."

Dr. Wilson leaned forward. "I'm here for *you,* Jacob. If you want to draw pictures or play on the castle or talk or leave—it's up to you. Do you want to talk?"

Jacob stared at him. "Mama thinks I lie."

"I don't think so. You seem like a very intelligent and thoughtful boy to me."

"I just want to go home," Jacob said.

"What do you want to do at home?"

"Talk to Anthony. Jump on the trampoline with the kids next door. I want to hear Amanda Lynn read about Narnia."

Dr. Wilson asked a few more questions—did he like school, what was his favorite subject. Then he said, "You're free to go or stay and play or draw for the rest of the hour."

Jacob looked around the playroom. He seated himself at the table and happily drew while Dr. Wilson sat in his chair writing notes.

Chapter 16

This house which our Lord speaks of is the human self. Inside the house, human Wit is lord of the house and the ill-disciplined wife can be known as Will. If the house is run the way she wants it, she brings it all to ruin, unless Wit as lord disciplines her better and takes away from her much of what she wants. And yet her whole household would obey her totally if Wit did not forbid them; for they are all ill-disciplined and reckless servants, unless he guides them.

– Sawles Warde

Jacob ran into the house, joyful from sitting with the Lovard kids in the ruins, where fall colors now hung over the walls, excited to show Daddy what he found there.

Mrs. Lovard had sat in the grass with them. Jacob thought her stomach was getting bigger. It felt soft and comfortable as he leaned against her, her arm around his shoulder and all the kids piled against him as she read about the Pevensie children finding themselves in mysterious ruins.

"Like these!" Maria said excitedly, pointing to the walls around them.

With a nod, Mrs. Lovard kept reading as the Pevensie children explored the castle and found a chess piece—a golden knight with ruby eyes! Jacob gasped as the children realized it was their own castle, where they had lived long ago as kings and queens.

Suddenly, Ethan jumped up. "Hey, Jacob, what do you think that is over there?" Jacob looked where the older boy pointed. Something glinted in a far corner of the ruins. He scrambled to his feet, and ran across the grass to the far side. "It's gold!" he called.

The kids gathered around him. "Dig it up!" Maria hopped from foot to foot.

They all shouted and yelled as Jacob dug in with his hands.

And then there it was! A gold knight on a rearing horse with ruby eyes! Jacob beamed, then he jumped to his feet, waving and whooping. "It was a castle!" he shouted. "Maybe *this* is Caer Paravel!"

"Maybe!" They all laughed, till Mrs. Lovard said, "Come on kids, let's finish the chapter. I'm guessing Jacob has some homework to do?"

Jacob nodded vigorously.

Jacob raced in the house, elated with the find in the ruins. Mrs. Mole was making dinner. "Where have you been?" she asked. She glanced at his pants, with scuffed knees. "Young man, you had best take care not to tear the knees in your pants! Dinner's ready soon."

"What did you make?"

"Escargot," Mrs. Mole said briskly.

"Isn't that French for *snail*?"

"Indeed it is! I'm glad you've been doing your lessons."

"I don't want to eat snails."

Mrs. Mole removed her apron and hung it up. "You will not be eating *snails*. You will be eating *escargot*."

"But you said…"

"They are a *delicacy*, young man. You are very lucky to be able to have escargot, and I don't want to hear that you've given your mother any trouble about it. Now go wash those hands and change into clean clothes for dinner."

"Yes, Mrs. Channing," Jacob said.

"I'm leaving dinner in the warmer and heading out for the day. Let your mother know."

"Yes, Mrs. Channing." He ran up to Daddy's office upstairs, showing the knight to him. Daddy put a finger to his lips and Jacob saw he was on a computer meeting. But he smiled and beckoned Jacob in. "I'm on mute," he said softly, and gave Jacob a hug. "I'm almost done."

Jacob watched entranced as several men in suits talked on the screen about all sorts of big words he didn't understand, then laughed and joked a bit and said good-bye to one another.

"All right, Champ," Daddy said, standing up. He wore a shirt and tie and dress jacket and his gym shorts. He saw Jacob staring and laughed. "Nobody sees the pants. They're more comfortable. Time to get cheese for Anthony?"

Jacob nodded, telling Daddy all about the find of the golden knight as they walked down the stairs and across the big room. "You still haven't gone to the ruins with me," he said. "What if there are more chess pieces?"

"There might be. I'll have to make the time. I have a meeting with a client in fifteen minutes, but maybe Saturday." He opened the refrigerator. "What would Anthony like today? Looks like we have some Havarti." He took it out, slicing it and dropping ten pieces into the small plastic tub. "I've kind of gotten into this cheese thing," he said. "I read online that Havarti goes well with raisins and walnuts. Do you think Anthony would like that?"

"I don't know," Jacob said. "If he doesn't, I'll bring them back."

After Daddy sprinkled raisins and nuts on top of the cheese, Jacob took the tub and started out of the room. He was halfway across the wide floor between all the rooms when the glass doors to the back porch opened behind him.

"Jacob?"

Jacob froze at Mama's voice, not turning. "Do you know why there are pennies all around the fountain? And dozens of them *in* the fountain?"

"The kids were teaching me to toss pennies." Jacob stood very still.

"Could you turn around and look at me, please?"

His father's footsteps approached. "Faith, I had to tell you...."

"Jacob, turn around and look at me when I speak to you."

"Yes, Mama." He turned slowly. She wore a pair of red jeans and a long-sleeved black shirt and black tennis shoes.

Her eyes flickered to the tub of cheese and fruit and back to his eyes. "First, you will have to go out and clean up all those pennies. I do *not* want you playing with those ragamuffin kids and I *definitely* do not want them throwing things on our property."

"But it was just for fun—to see if...."

"I do not want them throwing things on our property. I will be talking to their parents about this as soon as I'm done dealing with Dan."

"Mama, please don't."

Mama squatted down in front of him. "I most certainly will!"

"Their little boy is sick."

"Does that give them the right to throw things all over my yard?"

"It's just pennies," Daddy said. "I'll clean them up right now."

"He's *very* sick," Jacob whispered.

"That's not the point," Mama said to Daddy. "They shouldn't be there *at all*. And second—where are you going with that cheese?"

Jacob said nothing.

"I gave him permission," Daddy said.

"Against my directions?" Anger flashed in Mama's green eyes—like the Red Dragon just before it blew smoke—and she stood up, turning to Daddy. "I explicitly told him *not* to take cheese to the basement and I have told *you* not to encourage him because I can guarantee he thinks he's taking it to Adrian."

"Anthony," Jacob whispered.

"Faith, it's not that big a deal."

"It's a *very* big deal and I won't have it!" She took the tub of cheese from his hands and addressed Daddy. "I need to feel that I have *any* say in my own home! I need to feel as if *I* am one of the adults in this house with some say." She marched into the kitchen. Jacob heard the soft swish of the garbage can lid opening and closing. The refrigerator opened and closed and the garbage can swished again.

Jacob's lower lip trembled.

Mama came back into the big room, glaring at Daddy. "Do not undermine me. Do you know how it feels to find I have absolutely no control over my own life, in my own home? That what I'm trying to do here is being completely undermined?"

"Yes, Faith, I'm sorry. I'll take Jacob to his room."

"I'm glad you knew that's where he's going."

She watched as they went up the stairs, hand in hand, and past the big book shelves in the hall across from Daddy's office.

"Why didn't you do something?" Jacob whispered. "Don't *you* get to make any rules in our house?"

"You'll understand when you're older," Daddy said. "She just worries about mice and wants a clean house. She's worried about other things."

"But we never get to do anything. Because you let her."

Daddy sighed and sat down in the chair at Jacob's desk. "You know Mama gets a little stressed from work. She'll only get more upset if I push her on this. So we just give her some space and let her work it out, okay? She'll be fine at dinner."

"But I can't bring Anthony cheese anymore. It's not fair."

"Look, I just don't have time to get into it over cheese." Daddy took his glasses off and pushed a hand through his hair. "I have to get to that meeting. It's with the big bosses and a new client. We'll have the cheese in the kitchen from now on. Invite Anthony up." He put his glasses back on.

"He *can't* come up."

But Daddy was already walking out the door, saying over his shoulder, "Get your homework done, okay?"

Jacob sat by the kitchen window a short time later, listening as Mama spoke sternly to Mrs. Lovard next door about that passel of children throwing things in her yard. "I'm sorry, Mrs. Shorter," Mrs. Lovard said. "I'll tell them not to do it again."

Mama wasn't done. Jacob's ears hurt at the things she said.

Daddy came into the kitchen. He stood for a moment by the window, listening, too, then turned and got an apple, smearing it in peanut butter for Jacob.

"My kids will clean up the pennies," came Mrs. Lovard's voice sternly. "As to the rest, whether you approve or disapprove of my children or how many of them there are, is not something I'm interested in."

Jacob heard the front door click, and Mama knock on it again—several times. Mrs. Lovard didn't answer.

Several minutes later, Mama came into the kitchen, her eyes angry. "You are *not* to play with those kids. That woman was very disrespectful."

Daddy said nothing. He poured a glass of white wine and handed it to her.

"I want you to go talk to her husband," she told him.

"Yes, Faith, I'll do that."

Jacob's heart sank.

"Why don't you take a few minutes to put your feet up in the living room?" Daddy said. "I'll get you something to eat if you like. The party's coming up and you've been working hard."

She nodded, and took the wine across the big wide room with the fireplace to the living room. Daddy put some apples and crackers and cheese on a plate and handed it to Jacob, saying, "Take that to your mom, will you?"

"Daddy, don't say anything," Jacob pleaded. "Their son is…."

Daddy put a finger to his lips. "It's okay, Jake. Just take this to your mom."

Jacob did so. Mama sat on the white sofa with her feet up on the coffee table, her head back and eyes closed. "Thank you, Jacob," she murmured.

Jacob ran through the rooms to the big back doors, down the steps and along the fence, ducking behind a bush from where he could see the Lovards' front door.

Daddy was already on the porch, facing Mr. Lovard. "I am very, *very* sorry for what just happened," he said. "I told her not to do that. This is not how my son or I feel about your family. It's just, she's been under a great deal of stress at work."

Mr. Lovard's big mustache moved as he spoke. "Mr. Shorter," he said, "my wife and I know a bit about stress. Our youngest is in treatment for cancer right now and it doesn't look good. My wife is pregnant and not feeling well. Your wife needs to know we still will not be at her door yelling at her for any reason and we expect the same in return." He paused for a moment before saying, "I expect this never to happen again. Thank you for your apology." He offered his hand, which Daddy shook. "Take care of that boy of yours," Mr. Lovard said. "He's a good kid." He closed the door.

Jacob watched Daddy walk down the stairs, shoulders slumped. His face was bright red. Jacob crept back up the back stairs and eased into the house. He ran through the kitchen, getting to the basement stairs unseen, just after Daddy came in.

He stood on the top stair, listening.

"I talked to him, Faith," Daddy said. "If there are any more problems, let me know and I'll deal with it. I have meetings." He went upstairs and closed the door to his office.

Chapter 17

Love alone will be laid in St. Michael's balance: those who love most will be most blessed, not those who lead the hardest lives, for love outweighs this. Love is the steward of heaven because of her great generosity, for she withholds nothing but gives all that she has and also herself.

– Ancrene Wisse

Jacob lay in bed, his window closed. Mama had taken him again to see Dr. Wilson. He liked Dr. Wilson, he decided. He'd listened to Jacob talk about Methred and the wolf and Anthony. Dr. Wilson asked about school. They talked about Mama being angry about the pennies in the fountain, and the Lovards and the stories they read.

They talked about Daddy's words to Mama: *You should give people a chance. Maybe Mr. Lovard is someone you'd really like to meet. Maybe you'd even like to invite him to your party.*

Mama had been incensed. *Never! He and his street urchins are not coming in my house!*

Daddy had shrugged and walked away—but he seemed amused. Jacob didn't understand. Did Daddy think they were street urchins, too?

Jacob missed listening to the stories each night. He turned his head to the window and the moonlight coming in. He missed story time. But he couldn't bear to have the kids or their mother see him. For more than a week he'd kept his light off so they wouldn't see him. He stared up at the consolations on his ceiling, naming each one to himself.

The Big Bear, Ursa Major. *Click!*

The Little Bear, Ursa Minor. *Click!*

The Dog. *Click!*

Jacob scrambled to his knees, flinging the covers off. Something was hitting his window!

He peeked out cautiously.

Across the narrow patch of yard, Levi waved from his open window and threw a pebble. *Click!* Jacob ducked under the sill, hiding his face under the covers.

Click! Click!

Jacob came out from hiding. He peeked up cautiously. Now Levi, Maria, and Noah were all in the window waving. Levi gestured for him to lift his window. Jacob did, his cheeks burning.

"Hey," Maria said in a stage whisper, "Aren't you going to listen to the story tonight? We're on the last chapter of *The Last Battle*."

Jacob bit his lip. Then he saw Mrs. Lovard. She got off the bed, several kids bouncing off her lap like popcorn, and knelt by the window.

"Hey, Jacob," she said, "Is it because of what happened last week?"

He nodded, staring at his hands on the window sill. Then tears began to roll down his cheeks.

"It's okay," she said. "No one's mad at you."

His lip trembled.

Elias joined his brothers and sisters and mother at the window. "We miss having you at story time with us."

Jacob clutched the black horse to his chest, sobbing now.

"Hey, it's okay," Mrs. Lovard said over and over. "It'll be okay."

The kids echoed her words.

When he could stop crying, Jacob whispered hoarsely across the space. "I told her not to. I told her Malachi was sick." He hadn't told Mama he was throwing pennies, too, he realized. "I should have told her it was me. I'm sorry."

"Hey!" Amanda Lynn appeared in the window, now crowded with faces. "You're just five. It's okay."

"But I'm almost six. I should have...."

"It's getting late." She winked. "Now shut up and listen to the story!"

Jacob found himself smiling and Mrs. Lovard was right. It was okay. He wrapped himself in the blanket and fell asleep on the sill of the open window listening to the Pevensie kids' adventures.

"Wake up, Jacob."

Jacob stirred on his bedroll. The stars shone overhead. Ursa Major, Ursa Minor, the Dog.

"It's time," Methred whispered.

Jacob sat up. They were alone at the edge of the forest.

"What do you think we're looking for?" Jacob whispered.

"I don't know anymore than you do. But I could see his eyes glowing in the forest. I could hear his breath."

Jacob rose carefully to his feet. They both wore soft-soled shoes that moved soundlessly in the forest. They listened intently, watched carefully. Suddenly, a stag flashed past them, just feet away, darting out onto the open lea that spread out for a mile before the Red Dragon's lair.

Jacob and Methred drew back a heartbeat before a great, silver beast flew by. They watched, breaths held, as it sped after the stag, its feet a blur. Halfway across the meadow, the stag spun, rearing, pawing at the air. The wolf darted at its throat, its side, its legs, in and out, drawing blood, until the animal crumpled to its knees and fell.

The wolf circled the stag slowly, waiting until it became still. Then he grabbed it by its neck and began dragging it toward the dragon's cave. Presently, it sat down and lifted its nose to the moon, letting out a long, mournful howl. It lowered its head and resumed dragging the stag toward the cave.

Methred and Jacob watched, hidden in the shadows of the trees. A red glow appeared in the cave's entrance. And bit by bit, the glow grew until the Red Dragon himself appeared. His head emerged, sending up a spew of flames and a hiss so loud it carried the long way across the lea.

Then its body appeared, followed by its long tail. It unfurled its wings —one stretching grandly and the other broken and twisted—and then bent its head to feasting on the stag.

"Watch the Wolf," Jacob whispered. "The Wolf has been helping the Dragon."

"So we deal with the Wolf first," Methred said.

Jacob nodded.

Chapter 18

Our enemies swifter than eagles on the hills have climbed after us, and there fought with us, and still they plotted to slay us in the wilderness.

– Ancrene Wisse

Jacob sat by Anthony's window. "I couldn't come down sooner," he said. "Mrs. Mole has been staying until bedtime while Mama and Daddy go out."

"I'm glad to see you whenever you can come," Anthony said.

Jacob considered himself lucky to have been able to sneak away this afternoon to jump on the trampoline with the Lovard kids while Mrs. Mole made dinner and thankfully, Mrs. Mole was just leaving, with instructions to tell his parents the *keh de buh* was being kept warm in the oven. She'd glanced at the smudge of dirt on his shoulder and, huffing "You really need to keep your clothes clean; go change that before your mother sees it," she left out the front door. Jacob had sneaked by his mother's office and run down to the Garden Room.

"Mama won't let me bring cheese," he added.

"I don't need cheese," Anthony said. "It's all right."

Sitting on the chair, Jacob felt his eyes blink hard, the way they did when he was about to cry. He tightened his lips. He had important things to talk about. He couldn't cry, not now when he was almost six. "But it's not," he said. "Daddy lets her. He always lets her even when he knows

Laura Vosika & Chris R. Powell

she's wrong. Like about Mrs. Mole."

"Is that really her name?"

"No, it's Mrs. Channing but she has a big ugly mole on her chin."

"Probably something she can't help. Or do you think she puts it on every morning?"

Jacob laughed at the image but he shook his head. "No, she can't help it."

"She might even be embarrassed to know you call her that."

"But she's not nice."

"God loves us even when we're not nice. It's hard to love our enemies but He asks us to, just as He always loves us. Sometimes surprising things happen if we can be the first to show love."

"I don't think I can love her," Jacob said.

"Try just calling her Mrs. Channing—even in your own mind. Just for a week. See what happens."

Jacob was doubtful, but he said, "Okay. I'll try. But Mama should have hired Miss Grace. Daddy knew but he didn't say so. He let her hire Mrs. Mo….Mrs. Channing."

"Hm." Anthony sat in silence.

Jacob waited, watching his profile behind the bars.

Finally, Anthony looked up. "It's important to respect your parents."

Jacob nodded.

"But the Bible also says, *A child shall lead them.*"

"What is the Bible?"

"A book that teaches us about God and wisdom."

"There's a *book* about God?" Jacob asked in wonder. He'd had no idea! He liked his books about space and animals and trains. He wondered if this book would look like those.

"Yes, there is," Anthony said. "And it says that *sometimes* children will lead the way."

"Should I do that?" Jacob asked.

"I think as long as you're respectful, yes, it might be good for you to talk to your father about why he lets bad things happen."

"What if he gets mad at me?" Jacob asked.

~ 154 ~

"Sometimes we need to take risks for things to get better. Just like Rolund did. And if things get better, your mother will also be happier, right?"

Jacob nodded, though a little uncertainly. If she were happier, would she let him bring cheese to Anthony? After a moment of silence, he asked, "Aren't you hungry? How do you eat?" He was surprised he'd never thought of that before.

"Sometimes God works miracles," Anthony said. "I suppose He has in my case. I simply do not get hungry."

Jacob tilted his head. "Isn't it impossible to live without food?"

"Usually." Anthony shrugged. "Throughout history, though, there have been some very holy people who seemed not to need food, if they had sufficient love of God. Maria Domenica Lazzeri. Alexandrina da Costa. Lola—or Floripes de Jesus. Antonietta De Vitis. Saint Theodulus of Edessa."

"None of them ate?" Jacob asked skeptically. "That's not possible."

Anthony laughed. "That's why it's called *a miracle!*"

"So miracles are things that should be impossible?"

"Correct. Which is why we need have no fear when we ask God for help. We can face much bigger dragons than we think we can."

"Is Mal going to be okay?"

"Have you been praying for him?"

Jacob nodded, but then added, "I think so."

"Do you ask God to heal him?"

Jacob nodded again. "Yes, but Mama says God isn't real. So am I praying wrong? I don't see him or hear him."

"But He hears you and sees you."

"But Mr. Lovard said Mal is really sick. He said he might not make it. And I still don't have a sister even though I've been praying."

Anthony reached his fingers between the bars and Jacob wrapped his own fingers in them. "Sometimes things do look dark," Anthony said. "Keep praying and we will see."

As Jacob came up the stairs, he heard Mama's voice. "He is *lying* to me or else he really believes there's a man living in our walls—and I don't mind telling you it creeps me out—and I'm paying you to help him, to figure out what is wrong with him."

Jacob crept up the last step quietly. Peering out across the narrow hall, he could see Mama's back in her office. She sat at her computer, *zooming* with Dr. Wilson.

Jacob inched closer, sitting on the floor with his knees pulled to his chest, listening.

"Mrs. Shorter," Dr. Wilson said, "Jacob seems to me to be a very normal boy. At worst, he has a big imagination and that's not a bad thing."

"He turned in a school assignment saying there's a man living in our walls," Mama protested.

"He seems in fact," Dr. Wilson said from the computer screen, "to have a great deal of wisdom, knowledge, and insight that's highly unusual for a child of his age. Mrs. Shorter, do you believe there's more to this world than what we see?"

"I do not," Mama replied firmly.

"Talking with Jacob is one of the things that convinces me there is," Dr. Wilson said. "Because he's getting that wisdom from somewhere."

"I would like you to *fix* him," Mama said.

Dr. Wilson rubbed two fingers against his black triangle beard. "I would very much like to have sessions with the whole family."

"There is nothing wrong with me or Richard."

"I'll be happy to continue talking with Jacob alone...." Dr. Wilson paused. "If *Jacob* wants to come and see me. But in my professional opinion, I can help him *and you* best by seeing the whole family."

Jacob crept around the corner, past the big fireplace, and ran up the wide wooden stairs, down the long hall to his big sunny bedroom.

He pulled two knights out of his castle, marching them across a green sheet and over a wide blue ribbon toward the hill he'd made by draping the green sheet over two pillows.

The water splashed cold against his ankles as Pepper pushed into the stream, the big wolfhound, Arran, leaping in on his left. The stream ran heavy and fast with autumn's recent storms. Pepper shook his black mane, whinnying.

"Keep going, Brave Pepper," Methred said, even as he patted his own horse. "We have a wolf to slay."

"Should we not have brought more men?" Sir Jacob asked.

The water climbed up to his knees.

Methred shook his head. "I believe more men will only alert him to our arrival. And he'll flee."

The horses clambered up the far bank. Arran shook himself, flinging water far, and they rode silently for some time, climbing the hill. Scouts had determined, they believed, the wolf's territory. Methred and Jacob set themselves up in a thicket of brush at the top of the hill, from which they could see the land on all sides. It would be a matter of waiting, watching —and Methred issuing his own howls into the night, summoning it. They hunted a deer and left its carcass near their hiding spot to lure it.

It was the second night, as Sir Jacob kept watch, that he saw the huge animal emerge from the woods below. It stood a long moment, the moonlight glinting off its back, lighting up a ridge of silver fur.

It was even bigger than Jacob remembered. He suddenly questioned his own strength. But he steeled himself. He was here to do whatever it took—to pay any price—to stop this beast harming children. Arran watched through the tangle of leaves, before rising slowly, silently, to his feet.

Below, the wolf lifted its nose, smelling the air. It turned its head toward the carcass on the hill.

Hidden by the brush, Jacob nudged Methred softly. He came away without a sound. Jacob's heart pounded. He might not be going home. Was it Father Antoine who had talked to him about giving his all, even his life, for the sake of others? The dragon and the wolf were terrorizing the villagers, killing them, even killing children.

They must be stopped. Jacob's jaw clamped tight as his fingers gripped the hilt of his sword. He would do what it took.

But he was glad to have Methred and Arran at his side. Quietly, they moved apart, each to a small gap in the foliage, fifteen feet apart. Arran moved even farther, to where the brush circled to one side of the deer.

The wolf sprang suddenly up the hill, the moon flashing on its back and in moments, was hunkered down, digging into the deer. Jacob leaped out, his sword swinging.

The wolf's yellow eyes met his. Its lip lifted in a snarl, revealing two long incisors. It sprang, meeting him just beyond the dead deer, before his sword could come down fully. It toppled him to the ground on his back and gripped his left shoulder, shaking fiercely. He could feel the pressure of its teeth, trying to break through his heavy leather armor. He couldn't maneuver his sword. He hefted it, slamming the hilt into the side of the wolf's head, dislodging its teeth.

Now Methred was on it, shouting, as Jacob scrambled to his feet and Arran snarled, diving in and snapping at its hind quarters.

The wolf ignored them, its tail thrashing, diving for Jacob's throat. Jacob swung again, the hilt and his hand going into the open jaws. Methred swung, and the wolf drew back, its teeth scraping the back of Jacob's hand and his fingers.

It turned on Methred, while Arran lunged at its side and Jacob circled in, watching for an opening. His shoulder hurt. But he couldn't stop. He couldn't leave Methred, with the wolf suddenly leaping, lunging, as Methred danced backward, wheeling his sword.

For a heartbeat, the wolf's side was exposed. Jacob drove in. Arran attacked. And moments later, the wolf lay dead.

Panting, Methred stared at it. His breath came in heavy heaves, matching Jacob's own. Finally, he looked up. Their eyes met in the moonlight. "Well done, Sir Jacob." He smiled, suddenly, his teeth white in the moonlight. "We are a step closer to protecting our people."

Chapter 19

The pelican is a bird so ill-humored and so angry that it often kills its own chicks in fury when they anger it; and then soon after it becomes very sorry and makes a great lamentation and strikes itself with the bill it has just killed its chiks with....This bird, the pelican, is the ill-humored anchoress; her chicks are her good works, which she often kills with the bill of acute anger. ... Anger, while it lasts, so blinds the heart that she cannot know the truth.

– Ancrene Wisse

Jacob climbed up on his chair, rubbing his sore shoulder. It had been several nights since they'd eaten together. Mama and Daddy ate out for their anniversary and had business dinners with colleagues and a welcome party for Daddy at his new office. It was a relief not to have to eat dinner with Mrs. Channing and her chin mole. So far, trying to show her *love* wasn't doing anything. She only seemed angrier.

"Your shoulder hurt, Bud?" Daddy asked.

Jacob shrugged. He didn't want Mama knowing he'd been with the Lovard kids again.

"Something happen?" Daddy asked. He leaned over to lift the sleeve of Jacob's t-shirt. He frowned. "That's quite a bruise."

Mama brought a steaming pot out from the kitchen, glancing at his shoulder and frowning, too. "Jacob, how did this happen?" She saw, then, the back of his hand and fingers. Setting the pot down swiftly on a trivet, she took his hand, examining the scratches there.

"I was just running around the back yard," he said. It was true—he just didn't say it was the *Lovard's* back yard. "I missed a step and fell." He didn't say it was on the trampoline that he missed his step and fell to the ground.

"Hm." Mama let go of his hand and lifted the lid from the pot. Steam rose and it smelled as good as the steaming pots hanging over the fireplaces in Methred's kitchen. "Did Mrs. Channing get some antibiotic on it?"

"Yes, Mama," he said, as she ladled a rich serving of meat and vegetables onto his plate. "Ribs and carrots?" he asked.

"*Carre de boeuf* and *carrotes julienne*," Mama corrected, sounding like Miss DuBois and Mrs. Channing.

"Which is French for ribs and carrots," Daddy said.

"*Thinly* sliced carrots. And an educated man will know, when he is told he's getting *carre de boeuf and carrotes julienne* what that means," Mama said.

Jacob pushed at the rack of ribs on his plate. He hated ribs. He could never cut them without causing a mess.

"Use your knife, Jacob. Cut carefully. You have to eat."

"There are some people who don't," Jacob said.

"Who don't eat?" Mama sliced at her ribs. "Yes, they're called poor people and they're unhappy because they're hungry and we don't approve of starvation in this house."

"No, people who don't get hungry. Ever. They just don't eat."

Mama put a bit of meat into her mouth, chewing slowly before saying, "That's not possible. People *have* to eat."

"That's why it's a miracle."

"No, there's no such thing as miracles. Why don't you tell me who these people are who never eat."

"Maria Domenica Lazzeri. Alex...Alexandria...no Alexandrina da Coasta. Lola."

"*Lola*?" Mama raised a skeptical eyebrow.

Daddy frowned at him.

"Floripes de Jesus is her other name," Jacob said. "And Antonietta de Vitis and Saint Theodulus of Edessa!" He finished victoriously, surprised he had remembered such difficult names. Maybe that was a miracle?

"You're making things up," Mama said. "I've never heard of any of those people. People have to eat. You'll starve to death in a month if you don't eat."

"Say those names again." Daddy pulled out his phone.

"Maria Domenica Lazzeri." Jacob was surprised he could remember the name a second time.

Daddy punched into his phone, read it for a bit, then looked up at Mama. "He's right."

Mama's fork hit her plate.

"Who else, Buddy?"

"Alexandrina da Costa."

They went through the whole list—all the names Jacob could remember.

Mama became pale against her dark hair. "Stop it," she said.

"No, Faith, he's right. These people lived for years with nothing but the Eucharist."

"It's people making it up. That didn't happen."

"That's why it's called a miracle, Mama. It shouldn't be able to happen but it does."

"No, Jacob." She sounded angry. "It *didn't* happen. It's people telling lies to...to convince people of things that aren't true."

"But how did he know these names?" Daddy asked. "Whether these reports are true or not, how does he know these names?"

Mama stared at him. "It was those Lovards filling your head with their Catholic nonsense."

Jacob said nothing.

"Well?" she asked. "How did you know? Was it them?" She lifted her glass of white wine.

"Anthony," he whispered. "I told him I couldn't bring him cheese and I thought he'd be hungry and he said he's not and he told me about them."

"*Anthony*." She set the glass down hard enough Jacob feared its slender stem would break. "Does not *exist*."

Jacob watched Mama carefully. Anthony was right. She wasn't angry. She was scared.

"It's okay, Mama," he said. "He's not scary. He's good."

"He doesn't *exist*," Mama said.

"Maybe not," Daddy pointed out, "and yet Jake knows these names which he couldn't possibly know."

"Come downstairs right now," Mama said. "Show me or stop telling these lies."

Something fluttered in Jacob's stomach. Mama would throw Anthony out. If she didn't like pennies in her fountain, she would be *very* upset with Anthony in her basement. He said a prayer to the Unknown God that Mama would not do that.

☩

Anthony knelt in front of the crucifix that glowed in the light of a candle. The candle seemed to go out only at night when he stretched out for a few hours between prayers on his cot. Miracles indeed. He stared at the Crucifix.

How long have I been down here? He asked. *You know I want to be home with You. But You must have work for me still to do here or You would have called me by now.*

He stared at the Crucifix. Slowly, visions formed and came to him. The dim cell disappeared as he stood in a cloud or mist of some sort, Jesus at his side. He saw the Shorter family standing by a fountain with a rearing red stone horse, Richard and Faith smiling, holding hands. In her arm, Faith cradled a little girl dressed in a long baptismal gown, with red hair. He knew her name was Ava.

Jacob gave her a kiss on the head, beaming up at his mother.

Next door, the Lovards came out onto their back porch, one child after another. Last of all came Mrs. Lovard, her stomach large and Malachi sitting on her hip, beaming at all of them.

"He's better!" the children shouted at the Shorters.

Mrs. Lovard came to the fence, meeting Mrs. Shorter there.

"He's in remission," Mr. Lovard said. "It's completely gone."

Anthony felt the touch of a hand on his shoulder, and turned to look into the deep brown eyes, full of warmth, that he loved so deeply. He wanted more than anything to be there, to really, finally, be there with Jesus, with God.

Time stood still as he seemed to see all eternity before him and all the good done by billions and billions of prayers.

He hung suspended in time, wanting to be in his eternal home.

I still have work for you here. Jacob needs you. Ava needs you. Malachi needs you. You are making a difference to all these lives, right where you are.

Thy will be done, Anthony replied.

Jacob did need him. Christ hung on a cross. He could certainly hang out in his beloved cell a little while longer. The vision remained, surrounding him with sweet aromas and the sights and sounds of Heaven, immersing him in joy, dead to the world around him.

Jacob stood at the panel that hid Anthony's cell. Mama would be furious. But he did as he was told. He knocked softly on the panel. Anthony did not open the window. Jacob was perplexed. Anthony always opened the window, often before he even knocked.

"There is nothing there," Mama said. "I am very disappointed that you have been lying to me."

Jacob stared at the wall that always slid open to reveal the bars.

"If there's a room here," said Daddy, "there must be another entrance." He left the Garden Room and Jacob could hear him tapping and patting and knocking on walls.

Thy Will Be Done.

"There is no one living in our walls," Faith said. "He's lying." She stared at Jacob. "Make him come out if he's here."

"Anthony?" Jacob called. He didn't think Anthony would leave him in the lurch like this. Anthony would never do that to him. Maybe he was sleeping very soundly in there. Jacob was glad. He didn't want Mama kicking Anthony out.

What would you do for the sake of others? He was willing to have Mama mad at him to protect Anthony, he thought.

Daddy came back in. "There's nothing there, Faith. But you know, it's imagination, nothing more. He's not *lying.*"

"Whatever it is, I do not want to *ever* again hear this story." She marched out.

As they listened to her footsteps go up the stairs, Daddy furrowed his eyebrows. "How *did* you know those names?"

Anthony emerged from the vision, full of joy. His heart felt ready to burst with the warmth of having been so near God. For the day when he could be with Him always!

The voices came to him through the wall. It was Richard Shorter's voice. "You must have heard them at school. Did Miss DuBois or Mrs. Channing tell you about them?"

There was a moment's silence before Jacob said, "Yes, Daddy. Miss DuBois told me about them."

"Amazing stories," Daddy said. "Maybe Hamlet was right. Maybe there really are more things than we dream of in this world."

Anthony felt the sudden urge, the pressure on his mind, that told him he must pray. *Courage.*

Give Jacob courage, he prayed. He stared up at the Crucifix, praying it over and over.

"Daddy?" Jacob said. His heart fluttered. He was scared. But something told him he must do this. He had told Anthony he would be willing to do what it took to help others. And Anthony thought this would help.

"Yes?"

"You said we do what Mama wants so we have peace."

Daddy was silent for a minute before saying, "And?"

Jacob bit his lips together for just a moment. He didn't want Daddy to be mad at him, too. Daddy was bigger than Mama. It terrified him to think of Daddy getting as angry as Mama did.

"Is it peace if Mama is always mad?" he whispered.

He thought he saw Daddy's cheeks turn red. He wanted to crawl away, run upstairs under his bed and hide. But he spoke up. "It's the little things," he said. "First it's the little things. Then it's really big things. Important things."

Daddy turned to look hard at the panel that hid Anthony's cell. He touched it, moving his hand around. Finally he turned back to Jacob. "A five-year-old doesn't know these things. I think perhaps you really do have a Saint in your Cellar. Because you couldn't know that on your own and I'm sorry to say, you didn't learn it from me."

His cheeks flushed. Jacob was sure now that his face was red. His shoulders slumped as they had when he walked away from the Lovard's porch, with Mr. Lovard watching him. He looked for a moment as if he might cry. "Let's go." He held out his hand. Together, they left the Garden Room.

Jacob was grateful to take his bath early. He wondered about the life of the boy on the other side. Did he live in a big house, too? Was his life the opposite of Jacob's? Was his Mama happy and his Daddy upset? Or were they all happy? Maybe the boy on the other side of the tub had a little sister. Maybe he'd accidentally gotten the sister Jacob couldn't find?

Jacob got out of the tub and dried off, grateful to go to bed, away from Mama drinking her white wine in the living room and muttering in agitation to Daddy.

In his pajamas, he knelt on his bed to look over at the Lovards' house. A hallway light spilled into the bedroom opposite his. The kids weren't there to read stories yet.

Instead, a pale, little face looked back at him from the window there. It must be Malachi. Mal was the only one he'd never met. He was home from the hospital!

Jacob waved. The little boy's face lit with a big smile. He waved in return, then ducked beneath the window ledge and disappeared.

Jacob remembered his promise to Amanda Lynn. Anthony was praying for them. He scrunched up under his blanket and stared at the glow in the dark stars on his ceiling. Mama had told him the names of all the consolations. He stared at Draco the Dragon: the last thing he and Methred must defeat.

Mama said explosions of gas created the stars and everything.

Anthony said God put the stars there.

God, Jacob thought, *Anthony says you're there. Mama says you're not.* He'd said the words before, but he said them again, in his mind, *If you are, please help Amanda Lynn's family.*

He thought he must believe Anthony more than Mama, since he was talking to his God. His eyes drifted to Andromeda, the Chained Maiden. Her mother, Cassiopeia, was also in the stars. Mama said there was no forever—but she also said mother and daughter were in the stars forever.

Adults, Jacob thought, were very confusing. If they could be in the stars forever, then there must *be* a forever—so why couldn't there be a God who lasted forever? He spoke again to God in his thoughts. *They really need your help with Malachi. Could you help him?*

In the house next door, the hallway light winked off, leaving the world dark but for the glowing consolations above.

Jacob closed his eyes.

Chapter 20

Three foes fight against me. And I can still be badly frightened by their blows and must guard myself cleverly through your grace against the world, my flesh, and the devil…by myself I was a coward and weak and nearly fallen down.

– The Wooing of Our Lord

Lights went up around the house, put up by a dozen workmen—fairy lights, Mama called them—and three musicians sat in the big front hall in front of the fireplace, in tuxedos playing violins and a cello. Jacob wore his own tuxedo and shook hands and bowed, as he had learned in his etiquette classes, with Mama and Daddy's *colleagues* and their sons and daughters, several of them his age. They ate little finger foods Mama called "Aw dooves." She sparkled in red sequins and the women glittered and leaned in with flashing rings on their fingers saying, "Faith, what a *beautiful* home!" and they went upstairs to the ballroom where four more musicians played and the *colleagues* and neighbors—except for the Lovards—danced.

Jacob stood along the edge of the ballroom, way up on the third floor, watching, being proper and quiet as his teachers and Mama and Mrs. Channing had taught him. He bowed to a seven-year-old girl, the daughter of a *colleague,* and danced a V-N Knees Waltz with her, and returned to the sidelines, thinking of the splendid dances in Methred's court.

Two tall, thin men in matching tuxedos carried in a huge birthday cake on a silver platter and everyone sang and Jacob blew out the candles. He was six now!

"What do you want to be when you grow up?" One of the *colleagues* sat down on a window seat in front of him. He held out his hand to shake Jacob's. "Brett Childers."

Jacob executed a bow. "Sir, I would like to conquer the Red Dragon."

Mama stepped up beside him in her sequined red dress, placing a hand full of glittering garnet rings on his head, and laughed. "Wouldn't we all like to conquer dragons! Jacob was accepted at the Academy and we expect he'll do well there and go on to one of the good high schools. Perhaps some sports—maybe tennis or golf—and civic volunteering that will help him get into one of the Ivies." She smiled down at him. "So many choices, Jacob! Law, medicine, business! Law is always a good entrance into politics, of course and there are certainly dragons to be fought there!"

"If you like dragons," said a large man with silver hair, "it's a shame Michael couldn't be here. He would love to talk to you about dragons."

Mama smiled. "Michael? Who is Michael?"

The big man squatted down in front of Jacob, meeting him eye to eye. "You live next door to a world-class expert on dragons! He gives talks all over the country. It started with…."

"I'm sorry," said Mama. "What do you mean?" She blinked several times, a smile stuck on her face.

The man stood up, smiling at her. "Michael Lovard."

"Yes?" Mama said. "Next door? With all the kids?"

"You didn't know?" The man laughed. "Of course he didn't make a point of it. Not that he doesn't have plenty else on his mind with Mal and his speaking tour and another book due."

"What are you talking about?" Mama asked.

"You didn't know?"

Mama shook her head.

"He writes as M. M. Love."

"You know, the movies coming out," Daddy said, standing just behind the man. *"The Dragon of Dinis Powys."*

"The family next door? That's M.M. Love?" she asked faintly.

Daddy smiled. If a smile could look angry, Jacob thought, Daddy's did. He leaned close and Jacob heard him whisper in her ear, "Told you to invite him."

The man looked down at Jacob. "You should really talk to him about dragons." To Mama, he said, "Shame he couldn't make it. I guess with Mal being sick and all…. He's a great guy, whole family's really nice, good kids."

Mama tilted her head, smiling broadly. Jacob thought her face looked a bit red under the fairy lights. "Yes, that is a shame." She turned to Brett Childers. "What is your Sadie thinking of?"

As the heavy man moved away, Mama and the *colleague* talked about Sadie, who stood across the room in her red dress with a big white sash around her waist, while Mama kept her hand on Jacob's shoulder. He thought perhaps Mr. Childers wasn't really interested in what he wanted to do when he grew up.

"Jacob," Mama said with joy, "Sadie is right over there! Maybe you two would like to talk." She sat down on the window seat and pulled him close, whispering, "Don't talk about Meth-head or Dun Igliss or the Red Dragon." She glanced up at the heavy man, now talking to someone else. "And *certainly* do not talk about Anthony. It's not proper."

"Yes, Mama."

The guests left; the house emptied. Jacob stood beside his father in their matching tuxes, in the massive square hall between the front and the back doors, saying good-bye and thank you for coming.

Jacob remembered all his etiquette lessons in shaking hands and bidding the guests farewell as they wished him a happy birthday over and over. He was six now.

As the last guest left, Daddy loosened his tie and rolled his eyes. "Thank goodness *that's* over."

"Where's Mama?" Jacob lifted his chin as Daddy knelt to tug his tie loose.

"Not sure, Champ."

At that moment, Jacob heard a sound upstairs. He bolted up the broad stairs, following the sound to the bathroom by Daddy's office. It didn't sound good. Jacob pounded on the door. "Mama!"

It came again—like when he had a bad stomach bug last May.

"It's okay," Daddy said. "She'll be okay."

Jacob looked from the door and the sounds behind it to Daddy. He threw the door open. Mama leaned over the toilet in her sparkling red dress, shuddering, and throwing up.

Daddy stepped into the room, pulling her hair back. "It's okay, Faith," he said. "It'll go away soon." He turned to Jacob. "It's okay, Jake. Grab the Saltines and leave them in our bedroom, will you? Then go to your room, okay? Mama will feel better tomorrow."

Jacob ran for the Saltines, climbing up on a chair to reach for them. He left them on Mama's nightstand. But he didn't go to his room. He retreated into Daddy's office, clutching his legs to his chest on the window seat there and watching. Mama stumbled out of the bathroom, wiping her mouth.

"This is not going to happen, Richard!" she said.

"Faith, this will pass."

"I don't want to give up my career. I don't *want* a baby!"

"We'll be fine." Daddy put his hands on Mama's shoulders. Huddled in the corner of the window seat in Daddy's office, Jacob watched them in the hallway. "You can do whatever you want. You can keep working and a nanny can help us. We can afford this. The bonus I'm getting just from this case will pay for two years of a nanny. Or you can quit your job altogether and relax."

"I don't *want* to relax!" Mama shrugged his hands off her shoulder. "I didn't get where I am by *relaxing*."

"We are not destitute, Faith. I've nearly doubled my income with this

move. A little brother or sister for Jacob...you know he would love that."
Daddy touched his chest and leaned in close. "*I* would love that, Faith.
We can do this together."

Jacob pulled his knees tighter to his chest, huddled against the wall by
the window seat. A baby sister *was* coming. He didn't understand it. But
Anthony was right. A baby sister was here.

Mama yanked back. "No, Richard. I like my life as it is. Jacob is
finally in school full time and I can have more time to myself. The
appointment is tomorrow at eleven. I *will* be there."

Jacob pulled himself back into the shadows.

"Don't even think of it, Faith."

Jacob felt cold. Never had Daddy sounded so stern, so angry. What
was it Mama was thinking of? Jacob had thought, after the incident in the
Cellar, that Daddy would make things change. Instead, now he was mad,
too.

Thy Will Be Done.

Jacob heard the voice clearly. He drew a deep breath.

"Don't tell me what to do," Mama said. "I have every right...."

"And so do I. I have a right to my own child and Jacob has a right to
his brother or sister."

Huddled in the shadow of the wall, Jacob watched them in the hall.

Mama pursed her lips. "It's not your choice," she said.

They stared at each other a long time. Then Daddy said, "You are
legally correct. But it *is* my choice whether to remain *married*. It is my
income that bought this house and I will be happy here with Jacob."

Jacob, in the window seat of Daddy's office, clutched his knees even
more tightly to his chest, till his arms hurt. His left shoulder throbbed.

"Are you *threatening* me?" Mama's voice came out low and hard and
angry.

"I'm telling you *my* choice so you can make yours accordingly,"
Daddy said. "We want two different lives, Faith. If you do this, it's time to
part ways so we can each have the lives we want." He yanked on his bow
tie and strode toward their bedroom.

"Richard! You come back here! You are *not* going to divorce me and if you do, I'll sue you for every damn penny for child support!"

Daddy turned. He stared at her for a long time, while Jacob's heart pounded in his chest, before he said, "Is that what Jacob is to you? Child support to pay for a beautiful house?"

Mama stared up at him.

Jacob waited for her answer.

"You know he wasn't...."

"Do you have *any* heart? I thought you did once." He touched her shoulder. "I know it's buried in there if you could just let go of some of your scars."

She shrugged his hand off her shoulder.

"Faith, please. Appreciate what you have." He stared at her a long moment. "Before it's too late."

She marched into their bedroom, not answering.

Jacob curled into a ball. Tears stung at the corners of his eyes and trickled down his cheeks into the cushion of the window seat in Daddy's office.

Anthony woke in what he was sure was the night. He recognized the call to pray—an urgent call. He climbed from his cot and knelt beneath the crucifix. The candle shed a halo around it.

He prayed throughout the night.

"Well done, Sir Jacob." Father Antoine appeared at his side as he knelt in the chapel. They rode out early on the morrow for the big battle against the Dragon. "You have slain the wolf. The people have taken great hope and even now a dozen monks pray as you go out to meet the dragon."

"Thank you, Father," Jacob said. "But Father, the Dragon seems just as big and strong. In some ways, stronger. Is it getting help from somewhere else?"

Father Antoine sat down at his side. "No, Jacob. It is simply that when creatures—people or beasts—are cornered, when they're the weakest, when they're the most scared of losing everything—that is when, for a moment they fight the hardest and thus may *seem* the strongest."

Jacob sat down and together they stared silently at the altar for several minutes before Jacob asked, "Do you have a prayer, a blessing, for our success?"

Father Antoine stared at the altar for another minute before he spoke. "I have seen two visions of what may be. There will be endless battles in which many men will die. Your three captains will die tomorrow. The Red Dragon may be conquered or may not."

The three captains were older men. Each had a wife and children. "I do not like that vision," Jacob said. "What of the other?"

"I believe *you* are the only one who can conquer the Red Dragon," Father Antoine said.

"Why me?" Jacob asked.

Father Antoine drew his eyebrows together in thought. "Perhaps there is some connection? It was when you appeared, as a baby, that the Dragon seemed to grow in strength, to develop its ravenous hunger. There are more things in this world than we can understand."

"So you believe I can conquer it?"

Father Antoine nodded. "That was my other vision. Your captains will be spared. But it will be at great personal cost to yourself." He turned finally, from the altar, to look at Jacob. "Are you ready for that?"

Jacob thought of Rolund. "I will pay any price."

"Will you pay the ultimate price?"

"I will pay any price it takes to bring peace to Dun Aoibhneas. I will die to protect these children if that's what it takes. Do you know from your vision what I must do?"

Father Antoine made the sign of the Cross over his bowed head. "Go with your heart. Do not be afraid of what is to come."

Jacob bowed his head before the altar. *God,* he prayed, *be with me. I will do whatever it takes to stop the Red Dragon.*

Jacob rose and together he and the priest walked down to the courtyard. Jacob mounted his steed and saluted Father Antoine as he rode out to face the Red Dragon, already soaring in the blue morning sky.

Chapter 21

So it is in the spiritual fight against the devil: his whole intent is to separate hearts, to take away the love that holds people together. For when love lies dead, then they are sundered and the devil goes among them immediately and kills on every side.

– Ancrene Wisse

Jacob woke from vivid dreams of a little girl in danger. He was in his bed. He couldn't remember how he'd gotten there. He thought he must have fallen asleep on the window seat in Daddy's office. The black horse was tucked up against his chest, under his arm. He sat up, and the fight—his parents' fight—came back to him.

He jumped out of bed, running down the hall. He skidded to a stop in front of the book cases, looking down over the banister. The ugly Mrs. Channing stood by the big fireplace with Mama, who wore her long red cardigan.

"Good morning, Mrs. Channing!" Mama said. She almost sang. "Thanks for making arrangements to be here. Jacob is always so happy to have you here!"

"No I'm not!" Jacob shouted over the rail.

Mama spun, looking up. "Jacob!"

"What are you going to do?" Jacob demanded.

"Do? What do you mean?" Mama laughed—but Jacob saw she was

scared.

"Manners, young man!" Mrs. Channing said.

"What are you doing to my baby sister?"

Mama turned pale. "Jacob, how dare you!"

Jacob bolted down the stairs, shouting, "I want my sister! I want her! Don't you do anything to her!"

He threw himself at Mama.

Mrs. Channing grabbed at him, saying sternly, "That will be all of that, young man!"

"Leave me alone!" Jacob twisted out of the old woman's grip and advanced on Mama, who backed away.

"You stop this, Jacob," she ordered. "There is no sister and you are embarrassing me in front of Mrs. Channing."

"What is going on down there?" Daddy came from his office, his hair standing on end.

"There's a sister," Jacob insisted. "Anthony told me so."

Mrs. Channing grabbed his arm.

He tried to shake free from her grasp, sobbing and shouting, "You leave her alone."

"Let go of him!" Daddy pounded down the stairs.

Mrs. Channing shook Jacob's arm so hard it jolted his head.

"You're done here," Daddy shouted at her.

"I hired her," Mama yelled. "She's staying."

"Get. Out!" Daddy pointed at the door.

Jacob kicked her hard in the shin, and bolted out the front door, running down the stairs and onto Summit Avenue.

"*Jacob!*" someone screamed.

"Jacob, get up!"

Jacob shook his head, staring up at the red wing that swept over him. He reeled from the blow. The Red Dragon's wing had clipped him hard, sending him flying off his horse and crashing to the ground.

"Jacob! I need you!"

He stumbled, dazed, pushing himself off the ground. The creature soared aloft, its whole wing and crippled wing blotting out the sun for a moment. It hissed, breathing fire into the air.

"Hurry, Jacob! It's coming around again!"

Jacob fought the ringing in his ears, feeling on the ground for his sword, and clambered back onto his horse.

The great beast circled against the sun, and came swooping back, diving in closer and closer, one wing bent. For just a second, Jacob pitied it. Then he remembered the children it had eaten. "Fire!" he called.

Behind him, five hundred arrows let loose, aimed at the flying monster, a black cloud against the sky.

"Fire!" Jacob shouted.

Another five hundred let loose as the first group of archers nocked new arrows.

"Fire!" Jacob shouted. And, "Charge!"

As the Red Dragon crashed in at them, arrows in its body, Jacob leaned in and spurred his horse forward. He thought of Rolund, who had died to protect those children—all future children. He might die, incinerated on the Red Dragon's fiery breath. It didn't matter.

The Dragon crashed to the earth, skidding, wings flapping, breathing smoke and shaking its head. It bellowed, its green eyes glittering in hate and fury.

Jacob lowered his visor. He raised his lance and spurred his horse. If Rolund had given all to protect the villagers' children, so could he.

The Dragon sucked in an ugly breath and glared at him. It hissed, drew in deep breath and advanced on him. It flung its head, slamming into his left side, and flinging him across the lea. He landed, crumpling his right leg. His entire left side hurt. His face burned from the dragon's flames.

Jacob opened his eyes to bright light and blinding pain. He squeezed his eyes shut again; held them shut, listening to the sounds around him. Sensations crept in. Something burned—seared. He couldn't tell where.

Was it the Red Dragon's fire that seared his skin?

Voices murmured around him softly. He thought of Arbella and her children around Rolund. But it was different. He wasn't a knight. He was just a boy. He wanted Anthony.

Is he doing okay?

Voices came through his dreams and thoughts and pain.

Better than we first hoped. Pretty nasty pounding he took.

….ran in front of a car...

Anything you can do for him...anything.

Jacob heard the sound of sobbing before he sank back into deep sleep.

Methred danced with the maidens, lifting his chalice high. He threw his head back, laughing under the flickering candle flames, dancing over the scented straw thrown over the floor of the great hall.

Something hurt.

Jacob opened his eyes, hoping to see Anthony.

His father's worried eyes looked back at him. "You doing okay, Champ?"

Jacob nodded weakly. The fight with the Red Dragon loomed large. Where was Anthony? "Methred?"

"Just me, Buddy."

Jacob felt a warm hand in his. He sank into sleep again.

Methred stood at the head table, lifting his chalice, saying, "Sir Jacob landed the final blow! Sir Jacob has saved us from the Red Dragon!"

Jacob alone did not stand—he could not after the way the Dragon had slammed into his left side, buckling one of his legs, severely bruising his arm, and burning the side of his face with its hot breath just before he plunged his sword into its neck, drenching him in hot blood. His face would be bruised, too, for some time.

All the knights stood, shouting, "Jacob! Jacob!"

The minstrels sang. The maidens danced.

At the table, worn by the day's events, Jacob slumped in his chair.

"Jake?"

He opened his eyes. He hurt. He wanted to go back to sleep.

Mr. Lovard and Amanda Lynn sat in chairs by his bed. She held up the black horse Noah had given him, and tucked it gently under his arm.

"I brought my book about dragons," Mr. Lovard said. "If you want me to read to you for a bit?"

Jacob nodded.

"All the kids want to see you, but we'll come one or two at a time." He smiled, lifting his big mustache. "We can be a bit overwhelming." He started to read.

There was a castle, an infant who appeared at the castle gates, and a good queen who raised the orphan as a brother to her own son, Methred. There was a dragon who ravished the land. Jacob drifted off to sleep again.

Anthony knelt before the Crucifix on his wall, praying for Jacob, Richard, Faith, Ava. Often enough, Jacob didn't come down for days on end—but this felt different. Something was wrong.

He prayed for Faith.

Thy Will Be Done.

...he prayed for Faith.

He heard her voice outside his grate, demanding he come out, shouting...pleading...crying. He closed his eyes and prayed.

Jacob opened his eyes. Mama sat by his bed, her eyes swollen and red. She reached for his hand. He pulled it away.

"Jacob," she whispered. "You can't...you can't die."

He rolled his head, staring at her, at her ruby earrings, flickering red like the fires in the hearth.

Slumped in his seat, Jacob felt, more than heard, Methred jolt, staring at him. Methred shouted. People ran—priests, knights—easing Sir Jacob from his chair, carrying him carefully to his bed in an upper room. Physicians and priests surrounded him, doing all they knew how to do.

Methred bowed his head. "The people of our land are safe." Methred's voice floated around and below Jacob. "Sir Jacob—my brother! You cannot go! You can't! You *can't die*! I won't let you!"

Thy Will Be Done.
Anthony knelt before the Crucifix. The house had been oddly silent. He wanted to see Jacob again. He wanted to be in the Heavenly mansions, free of this small cell.
My beloved son, with who I am well pleased.
Anthony felt ecstasy, staring at the Crucifix, surrounded by the vision. *Jacob*, he thought. *Malachi. I need to pray for them. I need to help them.*
He could see Jacob in a hospital bed.
He could see Malachi in a hospital bed.
God, grant me these requests. Do not let my years here in this cell be in vain.

"Jacob. Wake up."
Jacob opened his eyes to stare at Methred.
Methred broke into a big smile. "We thought we lost you," he said.
"Still here," Sir Jacob whispered. "The dragon?"
"We have won," Methred said. "The Red Dragon is dead!"
"No more....children?"
"The children of the villages are safe now," Methred said, "and it is all thanks to you."
Jacob hurt everywhere. His head hurt. He closed his eyes. Blinding light surrounded him. "Well done, good and faithful servant." A hand reached through clouds. "Enter into the joy of your master."

Methred stared at Jacob on the bed for a long time. He felt un-knightly tears sting the corners of his eyes. They had been friends, brothers even, for more than twenty years, ever since the mysterious child had appeared at the castle gates and the Queen Mother had taken him in, her own child.

Methred lifted his eyes to Father Antoine, his heart tearing in two. "He has gone to his reward."

Chapter 22

But anchoresses, locked in here will be there, if any may, both lighter and swifter, and dance in such roomy shackles—as they say—in heaven's large pastures, that the body will be wheresoever the spirit wishes in an instant.

– Ancrene Wisse

Jacob opened his eyes. The lights were dim and the blinds pulled down. He felt the big, warm hand in his before he saw his father at his side.

Tears were in the corners of Daddy's eyes. "You're gonna be good, Champ. The doctors are taking really good care of you."

Jacob moved his head, seeing needles in his arms and equipment everywhere. His leg felt too heavy to move.

"Your leg is in a cast," Daddy said. "They had some work to re-set it. But they're very good at what they..." His voice got high and he stopped, and cleared his throat and said, "...what they do."

Jacob thought Daddy wasn't being honest. He closed his eyes.

Daddy took his hand away, laying Jacob's hand carefully at his side. Jacob heard his footsteps round the foot of the bed, and new footsteps approach. Whispered voices.

Swelling in the brain...

Can't get it down.

There has to be something….
Prayer. There's only prayer.

Jacob heard a sob from his left. He opened his eyes and rolled his head. Mama sat in a chair backed into a corner by the window. She jumped up suddenly, saying to the doctors, "You have to keep trying!" and grabbing Jacob's hand saying, "You can't do this! You have to stay here! You have to get better!"

Daddy rounded the bed. He gave Mama an angry look and sat down again, taking Jacob's hand. "Maybe your friend Anthony would pray for all of us?" He flashed a glance up at Mama, who tightened her lips and stared at the floor. Daddy looked back to Jacob. Things seemed to spin. "I mean," said Daddy, "if we have a Saint in our Cellar, that ought to be some pretty powerful prayers, right?"

Mama sobbed again, sinking into her chair. *There's no saint. I tried. He won't answer me!*

Jacob closed his eyes. Images and sounds swirled around him.

He saw Anthony kneeling in his cell. Bishops and priests wearing long robes and cassocks and tall hats came and opened the wall in the hallway, revealing a door. They ushered Anthony out into the world. "Good and faithful servant, you have done your work well."

Why did it take something like this for you to care?

Anthony blinked in bright light. The bishop blessed him, saying, "It is time for you to go home."

Let's hope it's not too late to show this new side of yourself to him. Let's hope he's coming home.

An acolyte stood in the hallway holding up a gold crucifix on a tall pole. Someone in a robe and funny hat swung a silver ball that let out sweet-smelling smoke.

I hope you can give up your cynicism—I hope you've been praying as much as I have.

He won't answer me.

The solemn procession, led by the gold Crucifix, moved down the dark-paneled hall and up the stairs.

Don't go. Don't go! I need you.

Jacob tried to reach a hand to Anthony. He tried to whisper, "Don't go."

"I'm not going anywhere, Champ," Daddy said. "When I have to sleep, Mrs. Lovard or Mr. Lovard or Amanda Lynn or Noah are right here by your side." He hesitated a moment before saying, "Mrs. Channing will not be your nanny. When you..." He seemed to choke for a second. "...come home, Miss Grace will be there."

Jacob smiled just a little. "She smiles," he whispered.

Daddy broke into a big smile himself. "Yes, she does and that's important. I should have insisted on it from the beginning." He bowed his head. "Jacob, I have failed you in so many ways. I'm so sorry." He lifted his head. There were tears in his eyes again.

"The doctors don't think I'm coming home," Jacob said.

"Of course you are." Daddy's voice caught again. He cleared his throat and brushed at his eyes. "Because your Anthony is going to pray for you."

They were silent a few minutes before Daddy said, "Are you okay with Mama coming to see you?"

"With my sister."

Daddy squeezed his hand. "It could be a brother."

Jacob shook his head, just a little, because it hurt. "No. Anthony said it's a sister."

"She'll be coming with your sister," Daddy said. "Jake, I hope you can forgive her. Sometimes...." He stared at his knees. "Sometimes people are broken by the things that have happened to them. This has shaken her. She's spent a lot of time.... We can make a new start. It won't be easy or perfect...but I think we can."

Jacob nodded and fell asleep.

Jacob woke to the soft hum of machines. A doctor and nurse consulted softly.

Not going to make it....

brain...swelling won't go down....

...leg...infection isn't responding...

Jacob searched for Methred. Methred was gone. Dun Aoibhneas was gone. It's beautiful turrets and banners, its meadows and river and Father Antoine...they were all gone.

...Nothing left we can do...

His leg hurt. His head hurt.

Jacob opened his eyes.

A man stood beside his bed. He wore a long brown robe with a cowl falling over his shoulders and across his back. He had a ring of hair all the way around his head, but he was bald on top. He sat down, smiling.

"Anthony," Jacob whispered. "I thought you left, too."

"My mission for the Long House is over."

"How did you know how to find me?"

"God tells me what I need to know."

Jacob reached out his hand and Anthony took it.

"Your mother has spent a lot of time in the Garden Room these past three weeks," Anthony said.

"Did you talk to her?" Jacob whispered. It hurt to talk.

Anthony shook his head. "I listened. I think she would have been too agitated to see me. So I just listened."

"But if she went looking for you why wouldn't she want to see you?"

"The human mind is a funny thing." Anthony tapped his temple. "Sometimes we *want* to believe a thing, but we're not yet ready to fully see what we have convinced ourselves isn't real."

A nurse came in, checking numbers on the beeping machines.

When she left, Anthony spoke again. "Your mother has been in the Garden Room asking me to pray for you to heal."

"Did you?" Jacob asked.

"Of course I did." Anthony laughed. "You're my friend."

"Then why do I still hurt so much? Why do the doctors think I'm not going to live?"

"Because the time has not been right."

"Why not?"

"Because," Anthony said sadly, "It sometimes takes people a little while to learn what our Father is trying to teach them."

"Did I need to learn something?" The pressure in his head increased. It hurt. He wondered if he would know he was dead—or if he would stay, a ghost, not knowing he was dead. Or would he be in the mansions in the sky?

Anthony smiled. "Not you. It took real fear, unfortunately, for layers of pain to shed off a heart that was hardened to protect itself."

Mama, Jacob thought.

"Unfortunately, instead of walling out the bad, we're usually walling ourselves in—into what becomes a dark, cold world." Anthony stood up. "Do you wish to be healed and go home to your parents and sister? Or do you wish to go to your real home?"

For just a moment, glorious white and clouds and beauty and peace surrounded Jacob. He saw a gentle kind man in a white robe. He wanted, more than anything, to be in this place that reverberated and hummed with *Love*.

"You can do great good for your father and mother and Ava," the Man in white said. "Or you can come home."

Jacob felt a stabbing pain shoot through his head. He didn't want to leave the Man in white. But he didn't want his parents to hurt. He wanted to meet Ava. He looked at Anthony. "I'll stay."

Anthony put his hands on either side of Jacob's head and closed his eyes. A pleasant warmth replaced the pain, like warm water in the bath tub swirling all around him. Jacob smiled.

Anthony laid his hands next on Jacob's broken leg. Again, warmth flooded him. Next, his arm.

"Jacob," Anthony said. "I'm asking you to understand a very big thing. Healing a body is easy. Healing the soul and mind are much harder. It's not all going to be perfect from here. There's much healing to be done and your parents will make many mistakes."

"I know," Jacob whispered.

"Change will not be easy for your mother and your father is trying, but he's still quite angry with her. He will have moments he struggles to forgive."

Jacob squeezed Anthony's hand. "I know."

"Just remember and be patient when things are hard," Anthony said. "Sometimes a child must lead and some days you'll have to show them the way to forgiveness."

Jacob nodded and drifted into pain-free sleep.

Jacob woke to a doctor looking incredulously from his clipboard to the numbers on the beeping, humming machines. He felt Jacob's pulse, frowning, and asked, "How you doing? How's that head feeling?"

"Good." Jacob pushed himself upright, dragging the heavy cast on his leg. "I'm better now. Can I go home?"

"You're Jacob Shorter?" the man asked.

Jacob nodded.

The man looked at his clipboard, at the whiteboard on the wall that had Jacob's name, and at the room number. He rounded the bed to look at the clipboard there and checked the band on Jacob's wrist. "Can't be," he muttered to himself, and to Jacob, "Let me talk with Dr. Anderson."

He left the room. Jacob could hear him shouting in the hall. Then running feet. Two nurses and another doctor, along with the first, crowded around Jacob, sitting up in bed.

"Impossible," Nurse Cara whispered.

"How did those numbers change so fast?" asked Dr. Anderson as he looked from the clipboard to Jacob.

More feet sounded in the hallway and Daddy appeared in the doorway. He stared at Jacob in disbelief. Then tears poured down his cheeks even as he laughed out loud. "Your Anthony came through!"

"Yes," Jacob said. "He came through on his way home."

Daddy stared at him in surprise for just a second before laughing again and crossing the room to lean down and hug him.

"Careful," Nurse Hannah said. "He could be...."

"I'm all better!" Jacob hugged his father back.

"We'll need to run more tests." Dr. Anderson scribbled on a note pad and handed the sheet to Nurse Cara. "Can you put that order in right away?"

Mama appeared in the doorway. Her eyes opened wide and then her mouth. She clamped it shut, moved it wordlessly, and finally said, "It's true? It's *true!*" She ran across the room and fell on her knees at the side of Jacob's bed, crying with big awful wails and lots of tears. "Jacob, oh Jacob—Jacob, thank God! Jacob, I thought.... Jacob, it's all going to be good now. I promise you."

Chapter 23

When a beloved friend leaves another, the last words he says will be the best remembered. Our Lord's last words, when he ascended to heaven and left his beloved friends in a strange land, were of sweet love and of peace. "Peace I give you; peace I leave among you." This was his love-token which he left and gave them at his departure.

– Ancrene Wisse

Jacob walked down the crimson runner in the basement hallway, between the dark paneled walls. Mama and Daddy followed him into the Garden Room. The panel was open, showing the bars of Anthony's cell. Mama and Daddy looked at each other.

"There *is* a room!" said Daddy.

"But there can't *really* have been someone living in there," Mama shuddered at the thought. "And how would he have gotten in—or out?"

Daddy left the room, turning toward the big room at the end of the hall. "Faith, come out here." His voice sounded funny.

Jacob followed his mother out. Daddy stared at a door. "It wasn't there, was it?" he asked.

"Well, apart from that first day we saw the house and a couple of times—I hardly came down here," Mama said.

"Neither did I," Daddy admitted. "But I *looked*. How could I have not noticed a door?"

"It's small," Mama said. "It matches the paneling. I can see how we just didn't notice it." She turned the small knob and the door swung inward.

Daddy found a switch on the wall and the room filled with light. There was an old chair there, a kneeler, a cross on the wall and two books next to the kneeler.

Daddy picked up one book. "It's another copy of Michael's book—the one we found in the big room." He stared at the cover for a moment before opening to the first page. He cleared his throat, swallowed hard, and read out loud. "Chapter Three. A History of Methred and the Battle against the Red Dragon."

Mama said nothing.

Jacob picked up the second book, covered in leather and dust. He pulled out the piece of paper stuck in it. As soon as he read it, he pushed it into his pocket. He gave the book to Daddy, who showed it to Mama. "It looks like a very old Bible," he said.

"But none of this is possible," Mama whispered.

Sometimes people aren't ready to believe, Anthony had said. Jacob didn't think it was the right time to say it. "Mama, can we have dinner?" he asked.

Mama held a plate with a hamburger—she held it out in front of her as if it smelled of stinkweed. Jacob grinned and swung his feet. It was big and juicy with onions, tomatoes, and lettuce on top. She grimaced as she set it down.

"It'll be okay, Faith," Daddy said. "We can have *duck confit* tomorrow. I'll make it personally." He sounded, Jacob thought, like he was trying to joke—but not quite managing.

He turned to Jacob. "We have some changes to make. Let's start with this meal." He folded his hands together like the Lovards did, even though he didn't do the squiggles.

Jacob listened as Daddy said, "Thank you for this food. Thank you for us being together. For bringing Jacob home. Thank you for the new baby."

Mama said nothing. She looked uncomfortable.

When Daddy finished, Jacob took a big bite of the juicy burger. It dribbled own his chin. He set it down and wiped his face. "Mama," he asked, "What is my baby sister's name?"

Mama looked surprised. "Did you know we already picked a name?"

"Ava," Daddy said.

Jacob grinned at him and bit into his burger.

He lay in bed as Mama read a chapter from Mr. Lovard's book, *The Dragon of Denis Powys*. She wouldn't read the story of Methred from his other book. It upset her. Jacob didn't mind. He didn't want to hear it right now. He missed Methred.

And he liked the story of this dragon, very different from the Red Dragon, even though he could tell Mama wanted to be drinking her wine to *unwind*. She tried too hard to make the story sound like something she was interested in—not like Mrs. Lovard read. Jacob didn't mind. She was trying. Anthony said it took time to change. He said hearts were much harder to heal and it would just take time. She was trying.

Mama finished a chapter and gave his hand a squeeze. "I'm glad you're home, Jacob," she said. This time, she sounded like she really meant it.

When she left the room, Jacob crept silently to the wall by his door. He could hear Mama and Daddy talking softly in the hall.

"Faith, I've been reading Michael's book. Do you know there are historical accounts of dragons? From naturalists and historians, from Charles Gould in the 1800s, from Marco Polo in the 1200s, from a zoological compendium published in the late 1600s, from...."

"Stop!" Mama said.

"...a nobleman named Christopher Schorerum in the early 1600s, from..."

"Dragons aren't real! Our son did not fight a dragon!"

"...the *Aberdeen Bestiary* in the 1500s..."

"This is ridiculous."

"There are historical accounts all the way back to St. Columba seeing the Loch Ness monster and to ancient history."

Jacob could see his father's shadow, holding up a book. "His story *matches* what's in the book."

"He must have had it in California," Mama said. "Maybe Julio's parents gave it to him. He must have been using that little room to read. And the Long's left the Bible."

"How was he reading a book in a sealed room?"

"I don't know *how*." Mama sounded agitated. "But there can't really have been a man *living* in our basement and there aren't dragons. We just didn't see the door."

As they disappeared down the hall, Jacob crept back to his bed.

In the end, people believe what they want to believe, Anthony said. Jacob smiled up at the consolations on his ceiling. She wasn't yet ready to believe even if she wanted to. He clutched in his hand the paper that had been inside the Bible. It said: *Richard, Faith, Jacob, Ava.*

He saw Anthony beside the Man in White. They both smiled at him.

From the walls he heard, *My Will Has Been Done.*

THE END

AFTERWORD

This story began with our visit to the Long Mansion on St. Paul's Summit Hill, in 2015, with a realtor. At the time, I (Laura) was very heads down in my research into medieval Scotland, and so was familiar with the tradition of anchorites—men and women who were sealed into a room for the rest of their lives, in order to devote as much time as possible to God and prayer.

They had a servant to bring food and take away waste, maybe a cat to keep away mice, and typically a barred window open to the church, in order to participate in Mass, and another open to the street so that they might counsel those who wished to come to them. (Of course, medieval times had scoffers and non-believers just as ours do, and there were those who might also ridicule them for what seems to many a crazy way to live. They merely considered this joining in the humiliation Christ Himself suffered.)

While in this house, we came across an odd room in the basement that was, as described, set in between the laundry room (which at the time we saw it was as described—not used as a laundry at all, but full of plants) and the big main room at the end of the hall. This 'cell' might have been used as a wine cellar or large ice box in days gone and could be entered from the hall—while having a grated window that looked into the laundry room.

Given my recent research, our first thought was to laugh and say it looked just like an anchorite's cell. *The Saint in the Cellar* was born, although with no clue where it would lead.

The quotes in Jacob's story are from medieval religious writers with whom anchorites would have been familiar. *The Ancrene Wisse* (The Anchoress's Rule, or Guide), *The Wooing of Our Lord*, and *Sawles Warde* (The Care of the Soul), were all anchoritic texts, books written primarily for anchorites to guide them on their spiritual path.

Revelations of Divine Love was written by Julian of Norwich, one of the most famous anchoresses, to record the visions she had in 1373.

Proslogion was written by St. Anselm, bishop of Canterbury, from 1077-8, and, in the form of prayer from Anselm to God, explores the rational basis for believing in God.

Chris began writing Jacob, a boy with very busy parents, lost in his own imagination. The question, we hope, remains: Is it his imagination? What did Jacob really experience?

There are more things in this world than we know of.

There are more things than we see.

Stories of Big Foot and Yeti persist. Millions have claimed to see or hear ghosts or inexplicable activity credited to spirits. There are stories of time slips, in which people disappear into another time and return with, in one instance, a handkerchief and stationary bought in that time, before later discovering the buildings where these things were bought, in our time, had been gone for decades.

There are, as M.M. Love's book says, historical accounts of dragons, including from Alexander the Great, St. John of Damascus, Marco Polo, and a number of well-known historians and naturalists throughout history.

Who is Anthony? Is he a man who has lived for centuries as his stories to Jacob suggest? Is he one of the deceased who doesn't know he's dead? Is he an angel sent to help Jacob? Or is he a figment of Jacob's imagination?

Are Methred and his kingdom real, a place that really existed that Jacob somehow accesses and lives in?

Or is it all in his world of make-believe?

From Tales of Things Beyond Our World

Conchobar was well-named. *Hound* and *desiring*. These things summed up his life.

He was my kin—and a sadder boy you'd be hard-pressed to find although of course, those were hard days. How many fathers were loving to their sons? Many were, in the hard way of warriors. But many weren't. Conchobar's father was the town regent and a harder heart you've never seen.

It was a hot July, the one that Conchabar turned twelve—three years after he'd come to live with my family, taking care of the stables at my father's inn—that the night was broken by the shouts of men and a horrible stench in the air.

I went to my window to see Conchabar standing in the cobbled street, staring down it to his father's home. Under the full moon, I could see it had burned. Guilt shot through me. I had done nothing to stop it.

A great gray animal, as big and shaggy as a wolf, padded up the street. Conchabar stared at it, unafraid. It came to him, so big its head reached to just below his chin. They stared at each other. The boy put his hand deep into the fur of the big animal and they stood a moment, nose to nose, before the wolf lay down at his feet with a whimper.

Conchabar stared down the street at the burned shell of the place that had once been his home, at the men shouting and yelling around it. He turned and went into the stables, the wolf following him. He didn't wait to see, as I did, that the men carried his father's body out of the house.

From that day on, the big dog was always at his side.

They stood silently, he and the dog, watching, the next day, as the priest sprinkled holy water on his father's coffin and as it was lowered into the ground behind the church. Conchabar turned to the animal and said, "I will call you *Fuascailt*."

When village boys taunted Conchabar in the market the following week, Fuascailt growled, baring its teeth. Conchabar was never again taunted.

In August, I brought food to the men working in the stables. Conchabar cleaned stalls while two of the older men worked with a new horse. As I set the food down on a table by the door, Fuascailt suddenly woofed at Conchabar.

"Hush, Fuascailt," the boy said.

The dog would not hush. It rushed at him, taking his sleeve between his teeth, pulling.

Moments later, the angry horse bucked, flinging off both its handlers, and kicked into the air right where Conchabar had stood.

The men, scrambling up off the floor, stared at the dog. "He knew," one of them whispered.

Fuascailt turned on the horse, letting out a low growl. The beast suddenly settled. It let out one last defiant *neigh* and then seemed to pull back into itself. Conchabar approached fearlessly. The horse tossed its head but at the low rumble rising from Fuascailt's throat, it dropped its nose meekly to its chest.

"There now, you'll be happier to let us give you dinner and a nice bed," Conchabar said, and led it into its stall and closed the door.

The men looked at Conchabar with something between awe and fear.

Within weeks, the boy and his wolf-dog were in demand with horse owners wanting him to work with their most spirited animals.

Through it all, I held a guilt and fear deep inside. I wondered if I was mad. And I thought of Athelyna's words, that July day I saw her come out from the forest, from a path that led to only one place—and a place no good Christian would go. *Is it evil to stop evil?* She had asked me, one slender black eyebrow arched, and a slight smile on her lips.

www.ingramcontent.com/pod-product-compliance
Lightning Source LLC
Chambersburg PA
CBHW060935180626
46817CB00004B/1567